Eternal

Tempest Saga

By A. Murphy-Parker

is really all it takes to improve the moods and lives of those around you.

It may pain some to admit the need to thank the Wedekind brothers, Barend and Wisse Wedekind, for their inspiration into some of my characters for this story. It could well be seen as pandering, but without their input then JW would not be quite a full-fledged character of his own. For example, he didn't used to be Dutch, *he was English*. Seeing the way things were, it gave me a refreshing look into the quirks of being a male teenager that I could not grasp, thus making the characters a lot more well-rounded and believable.

I owe it to my many beautiful, and wonderful, friends, whom provided me with support, offered comments, read, wrote, assisted in the proofreading, editing and design, and allowed me to quote their anecdotes, without which the story would have been a befuddled mess. It's amazing to think that it all began as several short stories from when I first started to write, with recalling back to past incidents, along with imagination (and pixie dust) so much of real life was put into this story...

As usual, my dear readers, hope you enjoy this novel.

To Wisse...

"Time passes, people move. Like a river's flow, it never ends. A childish mind will turn to noble ambition. Young love will become deep affection. The clear water's surface reflects growth. Now listen to the Serenade of water to reflect upon yourself"

- Sheik, Ocarina of Time.

Contents

PART ONE

First year

Prologue

"When shall we three meet again, in thunder, lightning, or in rain?" sang a young woman with freckles and blonde hair as she sat in the beaten up Cadillac on a hill outside Forres. Sueno's Stone stood high nearly a hundred yards away from where they were parked.

"Katherine, are you seriously quoting that?" snapped the middle aged woman sitting in the driver's seat, their eyes meeting in the rear-view mirror – a felt star shaped air freshener hung from it giving off scents of rosemary and peppermint.

"I was just saying it because we are here on this heath, like in the play," grumbled the young blonde haired girl, who squirmed in response and looked away bashfully.

"Oi, Mar, let her have her fun. Fair is foul and all that, eh?" laughed the older woman; Priestess Adrian was in her late forties and often joked a lot more than the other members of the order.

"Will you just get on with it? We came here for a reason; we haft a talk about the Galloway problem. We can't lose the strongest members of our coven! If we don't do something about it his family will leave the coven for good, it's terribly against the blood, alrite?"

"I don't see why we should be concerned, it's Richard who wanted to get married, and it's his decision if he won't be bringing their daughter up to be Wiccan," shrugged Katherine.

Adrian raised an eyebrow; "All's fair in love and war."

The happy couple in question sat in Grant Park having a picnic with their three year old. There was a delicious spread laid out on the red tartan blanket of pates and cucumber sandwiches. The woman had lovely tanned skin, dark brown eyes and a shock of auburn hair that matched her daughters. She also wore red rimmed spectacles and a silver nose stud...

Richard sat up and shook his head to clear it of his premonition. The phone was ringing but he took a moment to gain control of his breathing before he reached across his computer desk to pick up the receiver. He often thought about his wife, Bernadette, and that last summer before they had discovered her cancer. He often questioned his decision from the past. If only he had continued to practice Wicca maybe they might have had a chance to cure the cancer before it lost control...

"Dad! Phone!" Richard's daughter shrilled, her dyed brown hair falling in ringlets around her face as she refused to tear her eyes away from the television.

"Good Afternoon, Richard Galloway speaking," he responded, finally answering the phone. It was a caller in Dublin.... He had a bad feeling it was his vehemently Roman Catholic mother-in-law.

During his phone call, which he peppered in with concerned mumbles but otherwise gave nothing to the Irish caller, his mind wandered and he thought about possibilities for redecorating. The living room was huge, painted yellow and given a sort of autumn theme. Perhaps yellow was too bright? The curtains had leaf patterns and the wall had a leaf patterned border, and everything matched. The furniture matched, they were made of the same woods, and the computer was old and matched the television. Maybe more modern furniture was desired? A new television and computer would be great- if only he could afford it. Richard found it hard to let go of the things that his wife had bought for the house. The only truly noticeable change in the room since she had passed away was that the twin easels that usually sat by the back door waiting for mother and daughter to use them had been given to charity.

"Mary is dead," said Richard Galloway in astonishment after he put down the phone in the living room beside his desktop computer.

"What?" Asked his daughter in confusion, she had been sitting on the floor playing *Sonic Adventure* the whole duration of his phone call. Only registering the fact that he was on the phone to relatives by his obvious eagerness to finish the phone call quickly.

"You're grandma, the Irish one, she's just died."

"Oh, must be nice to not have a mother-in-law anymore," she responded light-heartedly, not putting down her controller.

"Melissa, can you come over here please," Richard ordered.

"Okay Dad," Melissa grumbled her reply, pausing her game before getting up to go to her father.

"Look, in an ideal world I'd be all 'oh there goes another one' but I feel a bit down. Just, God she's finally popped it," he added, leaning on his desk.

"I know that, she's really mean though, so why are you not happy Dad?" The young girl asked her father, tilting her head curiously, rocking on the balls of her feet.

"Because, if it were anyone else and she was here, I know she'd say that I am the one to blame for it. I feel like this time it *is* my fault. Do you understand?"

"Nope, she did try to drown me."

"They call it baptism," Richard retorted. He went on to explain in detail the things she already knew; why it was important to bathe a newborn child in holy water so they could become free from the power of darkness and brought into the realm of the children of God. The part of the notion of being saved from death in this method was completely lost, of course, on Melissa Galloway; who at the end of her father's explanation remained stubbornly convinced that the Priest at her Christening had held her head underwater way too long. It was this idea that left her afraid of water and unable even to learn to swim. Instead of being disrespectful, as she wanted to be and dismissing all the things he said, she shrugged and went back to her game. Richard sighed deeply. He couldn't tell if his daughter was being rude on purpose or just didn't understand because she was too young to. He felt that it needed a woman's approach and picked up the phone again to call his sister- Anne Galloway.

Melissa stood with her cousins in the hallway looking at their three young fresh-faced reflections in the hallway mirror. It was an interesting design for a staircase to have mirrored panels going up the side, and the two cousins marvelled at how well it hid the cupboard under the stairs with a fascination that only children can have.

"Where did you go?" beamed the older one with naturally brown hair who was two inches taller than Melissa despite being a year younger. "You vanished completely and all I can see is myself.

"Here I am!" replied the other girl, distorting their reflections as she pulled the door aside and popped out from the blackness with blond pigtails tied in cheerful pink bows. Melissa rolled her eyes at them. Her Auntie Anne was a divorced feminist who lived and worked in America – Melissa didn't care where but it allowed her cousins to have identical out-of-place voices and mature styles of clothing. They didn't wear white knee-high socks or pleated black skirts like her other female cousins that lived in Ireland. Instead, the two girls would wear name-brand designer jeans and t-shirts with slogans on them. Their socks were kind of hidden by matching Converses- they were dressed alike but in no way twins.

"Right, Melissa I have a present for you. A back to school gift if you will," Auntie Anne exclaimed as she burst into the hallway from the bathroom where she had spent what felt like hours putting on her make-up. The two daughters agreed that their mother looked lovely while Melissa became abruptly shy.

"If I will what?" asked the eleven year old girl in bewilderment.

"Well, it's a phrase, but that's not important. Richard wanted me to explain to you things that he finds difficult to talk to you about. It might have been something your mom would explain," Anne said scratching her head. Her daughters continued to play with the mirror door oblivious to Melissa's blushing red face.

"I know where babies come from, we were taught about it in Primary seven. My friend had a pregnant Barbie too, it was creepy, but Louise painted her hair pink so that was good. I -," Melissa stopped babbling as her auntie placed a manicured finger on her lips. Rather than authentic, hand painted, nice pretty nail art, that

Melissa's mother had preferred, her aunt had glued on fake red nails. Probably why she took so long in the bathroom.

"That's not it, you see my dear niece; I was asked by my older brother to educate you about a subject you don't seem to understand. Recently, you're sure to have heard, your Grandma Mary passed away. Do you get what I'm saying?"

"I think I understand grief," Melissa replied coldly, going from hot to cold within seconds.

"Ok, well I bought you a present, have you heard of Sabrina the Teenage Witch?"

"Oh yes!" Melissa beamed, quickly ecstatic and expecting something exciting to do with her favourite television show.

"Sabrina!" chorused the two cousins. Anne rolled her eyes at her two daughters. This was not the kind of way she wanted to tell her niece about Wicca but it was the last resort she had to broach the subject. Gently she took the young girl's hand and guided her upstairs to Richard's bedroom.

"Sit down," she ordered, kind but firm, and slid open the door of the built-in wardrobe. Melissa looked around the room and considered what had changed since her mother had passed away. The room was decorated to look like the sky. Blue walls, stars and suns and moons hung up around the room. The décor hadn't changed but the kingsize bedstead had been replaced with a simple double divan and all the furniture had been rearranged to accommodate a piece of exercise equipment and some dumbbells. The feel and scent of the room was different. It had smelt always of perfume and tobacco but now it smelt of her dad's sweat- like a bomb of maleness had exploded in the room. It certainly was not a welcoming scent to any female.

"Why are we in here?" Chirped Melissa, sitting on the bed with her legs crossed. She looked up at the bronze sun that adorned the wall opposite the doorway and smiled; it was always the best part of her parents' bedroom. That and the wind chimes that hung from the ceiling in the corners of the room- they were also made of bronze or something similar. While Melissa daydreamed, her Auntie searched through the wardrobe.

"I completely understand your problem with religion, it's not something that children tend to grasp as easily as adults, you sort of grab on to the part which sparks your imagination about magic and miracles."

"What has that got to do with Sabrina?"

"I'll explain that soon enough. Do you know where your Dad put your Mom's suitcase? I can't see it in here," Anne grumbled.

"It's up in the loft, with her other stuff," Melissa replied bluntly.

"Ah, fuck this then," Anne said finally with an exasperated sigh, after a couple minutes where she seemed to be frozen to the spot.

"That's a swear word!" Melissa gasped. Then the wardrobe seemed to swallow up her Auntie Anne leaving behind a whisper of Chanel No.5 on Richard's shirts and trousers. Melissa bounced off the bed to investigate, pulling the clothes on their laden hangers apart, there was scarcely enough room for a grown woman to hide in there.

"Here it is," Anne announced triumphantly, appearing behind Melissa – who frowned in confusion. The woman held a brown suitcase with red and white straps and an Irish flag label on the handle.

"You were in the wardrobe," the young girl probed.

"And now I'm not," her Auntie returned with a fairly creepy, straight, white grin. Anne dropped the suitcase onto the bed, opened it, and began to search through it – the suitcase contained mostly old musty, moth-eaten, clothes and books.

There were two items of direct interest to Anne; these were a thick black leather-bound Bible and a heavy metal Cross. She admired the Cross for a moment before putting it back and opened the Bible to flick thru the pages.

"It's a pity your Mom's clothes have so much damage from her smoking, otherwise I'd say they could be given to good homes. As it is, too many cigarette burns have made unrepairable holes in these garments."

"Why don't you call them fag burns?"

"Cos fag means something bad in America."

"Oh, that's not good," Melissa held her hands behind her back and rocked back and forth on her feet.

"Right; I take this text from Matthew 3:11," Anne began and coughing to clear her throat she read from the Bible. "I indeed baptize you with water unto repentance. But he that cometh after me is mightier than I, whose shoes I am not worthy to bear: he shall baptize you with the Holy Ghost, and with fire,"

"So, you can be baptised in fire as well as water?" Melissa asked in surprise, "That's awful! Why couldn't he wear his shoes?"

Anne sighed and realised she was getting nowhere further in trying to explain baptism. *I think I just instilled a fear of fire into this girl*, Anne Galloway thought to herself, *that's just great...*

"I don't understand, can you please explain what this has to do with Sabrina now?" Melissa babbled questions out in such quick succession it was a wonder any teacher in her school had not gone insane.

"Ok, another one. This text is from Leviticus 20:27. A man or a woman who is a medium or a necromancer shall surely be put to death. They shall be stoned with stones; their blood shall be upon them."

"That's one of the ones Grandma Mary used to read to me, her favourite was the one about Witches," Melissa mumbled, her face ashen.

"Yes, Exodus 22:18, thou shalt not suffer a witch to live. There are many lines like that in this book. I prefer my own laws," Anne put the Bible that had belonged to Melissa's mother back in the suitcase where it had been before and sat down on the bed. She took her niece onto her lap and spoke softly; "If it harm none do what ye will..."

"I feel like I've heard that before... but I haven't," Melissa whispered.

"It is the end to the Wiccan Rede, my gift to you is a choice, Melissa. All your life you have been raised Catholic, you were christened in a Church in Dublin, surrounded by all of your family, it was a normal infant baptism and the Lord God has protected you as Mary had wished. I give you the choice to choose another faith, to decide your own path on an alternative route, the gift I give to you is Magick," Anne had spoken slowly and calmly. Melissa listened, she drank in every word with more concentration than she would ever use at school. What came as a true shock to her Auntie was when Melissa didn't laugh but stood up and looked at herself in the mirror on the dresser beside the bed. Her eyes sparkled like stars in the dark cold night. Melissa spun on her heel and pointed at her Auntie.

"You did something like Sabrina, didn't you?"

"I did indeed. It's called moving through time, tempus motus in Latin. I simply ask the Goddess to lend me the power to move from one place to another. It's a matter of concentrating and controlling your breathing. The opposite of Richard's power, which is premonition, his consciousness gets taken out of his body where he cannot control his breathing and can only concentrate on the past or future image he is being shown."

"So my Dad has powers too?"

"Yes, my dear, many people you know have been blessed with powers. You might not realise it, but even you might have powers," Anne said clasping Melissa's hands in hers. "You might not remember ever meeting her, but there was a girl in your Gymnastics group when you were a toddler. She had the power to walk on her hands and could bend in any way with only a day of training from her instructors. It was miraculous!"

"She was probably a show off," Melissa shrugged letting go of her Auntie's hands.

"I'll tell you about the basic principles of Wicca another time, for now I think I'll leave you alone to think about it. We'll be having dinner soon," Anne said as she left the room.

"Ok," Melissa mumbled going over to the suitcase on the bed and looking at the contents with disapproval. She was precipitously outrageously upset with the world and something had to be done to slow her rage. Which drawer did her father keep his scissors?

Chapter One
Start of 1st year

Melissa had been grounded by her father for cutting up the clothes in the suitcase. Her Auntie, who was a fashion designer, said that with a little bit of sewing they could be worn again. It was something called 'grunge' Anne had said. Melissa had decided she liked that idea and spent the rest of her summer holidays learning about sewing and fashion from her Auntie before Anne, and her two daughters, returned to America at the end of the summer. When school life would resume for the children as normal.

Secondary school, the progression of education from primary school, it was called in Scotland. The idea was you were meant to be full of hope or excitement on your first day of a new school, but she was full of dread, Melissa stood in the corner shaking with irrational fear. She didn't want to go in, she was so scared, she was so anxious.

"Melissa, is that your name? Hey, I'm Jade Jackson, remember me? I'm your S6 buddy," Jade Hagan said to the poor first year girl, who had been hiding behind a garage outside of Forres Academy. "It's okay," Jade said with a reassuring crooked smile. Jade, a sixth year they had met before the summer holidays, a buddy assigned to look after the first years in their registration class. Melissa grew up to Jade's shoulder; she could see the sixth year logo in gold lettering, it said Forres Academy against a background of black polyester.

"How did you know I was here?" Melissa asked, shyly.

"My friend Edina said that she saw you go in here and sent me out to get you," Jade replied, with a comforting smile. Jade was tall, towering nearly a foot above Melissa in leather wedged boots, and had a full figure; Melissa wouldn't have thought Jade was a teenager if she hadn't seen her S6 jumper.

"I started to feel unwell, my heart was going super fast, like when I drink lots of Sunny D," Melissa explained, as she was gently coerced from behind the garage.

"I know that feeling, it's dreadful, and it's totally normal to feel that way on your first day of school," Jade murmured softly.

Melissa and Jade marched slowly across the road towards the school gates. Jade had Melissa hold her hand and she explained how she understood her feelings of fear.

Forres Academy comprised of large white panelled walls and black framework. It looked like a black and white dog when you saw the school map; which Melissa was examining as they stood in a cluster around Jade outside the school doors. There were outdoor benches, which were made from metal and plastic rather than wood. There was also several rather barren planters; these were made of brick and held baby beach trees- like the ones from their primary school, Melissa thought- as she watched her fellow registration class pupils stroke the trees for fun. Johanna, Alisha and Chloe had all attended Applegrove Primary school and Melissa felt they possessed an air of superiority above her- as this was the more sort-after school in Forres because it had the best access for disabled students. Melissa and Jordan, who lived next door to her, had gone to Pilmuir Primary.

Pilmuir had a disabled toilet and ramps but any students with special disability needs were silently rejected from attending. There was a third mainstream primary school in Forres, Anderson's primary, and this was the oldest school. It had no ramps, stairs, and still segregated boys and girls at the doors in the morning because of tradition. Yet, they did eat lunch and attend classes together so on that case it stopped being old fashioned, Melissa reasoned, thoughtfully. At this point in the story Melissa had not heard of the Steiner school- the author wishes this to be acknowledged.

"Gemma, why don't you come sit with us in class?" Johanna suggested brightly.

"You can too, Melissa," Alisha added, with a similar brand of chipper. It was obviously exciting for them- this whole notion of starting at a new school sent them into uncontrollable fits of glee.

"Melissa, what a pretty name," Chloe added, her glossy curly hair bouncing about, each ringlet with a mind of its own. Melissa, for her part, managed to inject some cheer into her voice as she agreed to this. Melissa then rounded on her toes to convey the boys in her peer group with an indifference to them.

Jordan Atkinson stood behind Jade and gawked; "You're b-you-you're beautiful," he said. "Just beautiful," Jordan mumbled to Jade, blushing while admiring her big bosoms... All of the boys in their registration class gawked at Jade and showered her with compliments. It was as if they had never seen a curvy teenage girl before in their lives- the four first year boys were only eleven and she was sixteen going on seventeen. Jade cringed inwardly but did her best to be nice to them.

"They've got no chance," Melissa giggled to herself. . Jordan Atkinson was undoubtable the shortest in their class. Jordan had a yellow pallor to his dark skin, short black hair and brown eyes. He was thin as a rake and, having lived next door to him for at least half of her life, Melissa knew that Jordan treated all women, who he had no relation to, with undying respect- and clingy adoration as he displayed towards their sixth year buddy.

"Err... thanks... Jordan," Jade mumbled. She turned her attention back to Melissa and smiled reassuringly. This took away from Melissa's anxiety and for a moment she forgot she was just a mere first year. She had gone from a little pond where she was a big fish to a slightly bigger pond where she was incredibly small. This was how most pupils felt as they progressed from primary to secondary school. Their perspective was thus; this place is full to the brim with strange alien creatures known as teenagers. They were mostly tall, and but some were smelly, hairy, covered in acne, easily confused with teachers- embarrassing at times- and called young men... Melissa cringed awkwardly as she watched older students walk past their group.

"Okay, now that everyone is here let's go into the school. Mel, you can be my wee sidekick okay."

"Okay," Melissa echoed, beaming, she linked arms with their buddy and they walked into the Turquoise doors together as a group.

Meanwhile, a group of first year boys were being chaperoned in the doors on the other side of the school by two S6 buddies- young men with scarce chest hair and weak facial hair.

"Did you see *baps* yesterday?" said one, as they shuffled inside the white automatic doors with their brood.

"Aye, she's helping the first years too remember."

"Oh, really can't remember since I wasn't at the meeting."

"Duh, I did cover for you. Mr Anderson and Mrs E were not happy that not everyone was there last night. Kind of important if you want to be a buddy to attend them, y' know."

"You're such a swot!"

"Eww! What is that smell?" a blond haired girl in their group unexpectedly shouted in alarm.

The S6 buddies shared a look. This girl was daughter of a member of staff at the school; she was exactly like her mother, they could tell from a mile off, the eyes, the face, and the tone of voice most importantly. Her name was Samantha Thomson.

"Ugh, is THAT egg?!" she declared, holding up the whole group for her outburst. They were standing in the foyer now; other students were trying to push past their group, mumbling and grumbling.

"It's my sandwiches," Perry Leach replied, "Mum made me egg sandwiches and... well she said I'm a growing boy," he blushed a little behind his glasses. He was skinny, but muscular, with black hair and pale blue eyes. He tried to regain composure but it was obvious he had been successfully embarrassed. Sarah looked away and got back to the business of chatting with the other girls in their S1 group.

"Okay, Pez, she's a cow," a first year boy hissed to him in a Dutch accent. They both were wearing dark green Applegrove jumpers. A ginger haired boy walked over to them and said hello; he was wearing a navy blue Anderson's Primary jumper.

26

"You're pretty cool saying that, my name's James," he whispered to the two boys.

"I'm Perry Leach, and this idiot here is JW," Perry added, with a grin, introducing his friend.

"JW, eh? That's mysterious?" One of the S6 buddies interjected curiously.

"It's actually Jozef Wouters, but Pez has called me that since we've met and the teachers caught on that it's my nickname," JW explained, his accent standing out so much that the girls who had not attended school with him were secretly listening to it.

"Ah, well, we'll see if Miss Cox and Mrs Bright will let you do that. Registration in the Drama department they sometimes switch over in the mornings, depending on who's running melodramatically late," the same S6 buddy continued.

"Mrs Bright will be your favourite though, wait and see," added the other S6 buddy. Both the teenage boys were appropriately sweet for minor characters but had a hint of mischief about them.

"Your hair is interesting..." James noted, nudging JW as they were directed down the Drama corridor from the foyer. The corridor veered off as you got to the end of the entrance hall; it was adjacent to the assembly hall and directly opposite the canteen.

"He tried to dye it blond," Perry answered for his friend. JW blushed profusely as they were again halted in the corridor next to the female toilets.

"Oh come on, what now?" Someone in their group shouted, her name was Jenny. A different eleven year old girl pushed towards the three boys, making it obvious what she was about to do, she looked him up and down and yanked his hair.

"Oh you are such a pretty boy," Samantha jeered, "look at that girls he's like a little princess," She added, pulling on JW's long hair.

"Samantha!" came the voice of a fantastically irritated woman who stepped into the Drama corridor from the female staff toilets.

"Mrs Bright!" The two sixth year boys said as one.

"I will not allow bullying in this school, I'm going to tell your mother about this behaviour the first chance I get. Apologise to the poor boy at once!"

"Sorry, sorry," Samantha mumbled letting go of JW's hair and doing as she was told. Mrs Bright was dressed in a knitted poncho, she had delicate features and wore her blond hair in a neat bun. She also wore half-moon spectacles and towered over their whole Registration class in her riding boots. She turned to the sixth year buddies with an expectant glare.

"Sorry, sorry," they echoed.

"To class!" The drama teacher declared. JW, James, Perry and their classmates did as ordered. The S6 buddies stood still as they received a short lecture from the teacher.

"Wow," a brown haired girl wearing an Anderson's jumper said. "I did not expect that," she added, as their group walked into the registration class.

"Me neither, sister," a red haired girl shrugged, standing in the group of eleven year olds with her friends in the middle of the room. They all stood around segregated into two groups of blue and green. All holding school bags and jackets.

"What do we do now?" James asked rather rhetorically. He took it upon himself to sit in the rotating desk chair in Mrs Bright's classroom.

"For starters, how about not sit there," Jenny answered him, turning her nose up till it pointed at the ceiling, she crossed her arms.

"Too bad you're a typical Applegrove student, otherwise I might have liked you," James replied, spinning in the chair.

"I have a boyfriend, so don't get that idea," she replied immediately, disgust clear on her face.

"I di'n't mean that..." James sighed, covering his face with his hands as he began to laugh. "...The look on your face!" he laughed.

"Ah, you," Mrs Bright said applauding as she pushed her way into the classroom. "Just, such magnificent acting," she added, striding over towards her chair, the blackboard behind her.

"What? Acting?" Jenny asked, appalled as she looked up at her Registration class teacher. All the fourteen eleven year olds and the two sixth year males stared at their teacher. James sat in his chair, his freckles seeming to vanish as his face reddened behind his hands- he removed them as his teacher placed a smooth manicured hand on his shoulder and pulled him out of *her* chair.

"You two, that charisma, such... chemistry!" she declared, looking to all the room that which she was- a dramatic drama teacher.

"Eww!" Jenny replied, turning away to sulk over to the group of girls. The boys giggled at the scene.

"I see you doing well, but on with this register that simply must be done. Please find a seat on the floor as standing in tableau is not very pleasant. Now, Alistair?" She began to call out names as she scooted into her chair. The sixth year boys took two chairs from a stack of wooden chairs at the back of the room- they were made of cheap plywood, no armrests and had peeling black paint. While they did this the eleven year olds, including James, sat down on the floor. Alistair Holmes, who was curly haired and sat beside Perry and JW, wearing a green jumper, called out to his name. As each classmate's name was read out in turn and they all replied "here" Mrs Bright gave little in the way of acknowledgement aside from murmurs and the movement of her pen over her clipboard. Until she got to the last name on her list.

"Good, now, I am sorry I might pronounce this wrong. Josef?"

"No, Mrs Bright, that was fine. Please call me JW. That's what all my teachers before have done," the Dutch boy (who dyed his hair blond) replied, his hand in the air.

"Ah, yes, I remember the husky sound of your voice from the visiting days. I am sorry, I shall write that down here now so I won't forget. You will not have to tell me again," she added, smiling down at him as she wrote the addition to her list of names. He blushed profusely.

"Thank you," JW muttered shyly.

"Welcome students!" a skeleton exclaimed happily as it was wheeled into the classroom from a cupboard adjacent to the whiteboard. Melissa and the other students had Mr Mitchell for science first thing Monday morning. Melissa's ears were still ringing from the bell signalling the end of registration. Mr Mitchell placed the skeleton in the corner and smiled, clasping his hands behind him as he observed the fifteen eleven year olds as they filed into his classroom on the second floor. The science labs were organised with three rows of high wooden desks and lined with six bar stools. The stools were plastic and plain while the desks were a dark wood and covered in graffiti- they also had two sinks per row. All of the sinks had deep basins and a tall round spout. In the front of each of the desks, facing towards the blackboard and teacher's desk at the front of the classroom- which was of waist height with old laptop and only one sink- that was next to where the skeleton was standing, were some plug sockets assumedly for any equipment and appliances. On the opposite side to the plug sockets were small lockers designed for the students to place belonging into during class. Melissa admired the classroom as the teacher told everyone to line up by order of their birthdays. They had already gone through this process in registration class so she knew that she had to stand in the December area between Alisha Stewart and Gemma Dingwall.

On another side of the school entirely, when science period had long ended, their German teacher Miss Duvall took the register after the mid-morning break and mathematics. Miss Cruella Duvall, as was ironically her full and proper name, looked to be in her mid-thirties. She had short a red-hair that curled around the bottom of her ears, and dressed like a typical teacher wearing a dark green pencil skirt and black tights with a blouse and cardigan. Her lightly freckled face and square-rimmed spectacles were not complete without her glaring blue eyes and mouth that was fixed in a constant scowl. Two sixth year males stood side by side against the wall adjacent to the door as she read out the list of twenty-five names. They looked so cool, thought the main character for this scene, JW, as he admired his buddies with awe. Arms folded, dressed entirely in black, dark stubble and strong manly faces. One had a small goatee and the other wore glasses, aside from this they were almost twins, matching converses and sixth year jumpers- the writing in a contrasting lime green.

Angela Quill? Here. Aiden Peterson? Yup! Connor Greaves? Here.

The list, as lists tend to do, went on...

Perry Leach? Here. James Mitchell? Yup! Samantha Thomson? Here.

"J-Jo-seph? Wow-ters?" The teacher said with hesitation, anglicising each syllable carefully as if to annoy him on purpose.

Jozef Wouters tore his eyes away from the young men in black sixth year jumpers and glared at the teacher. Miss Duvall had introduced herself as a Modern Language teacher yet she could not decide how to pronounce a simple Dutch name. "Yo-sef Vow-ters, Miss," he corrected her calmly, trying to be as polite as he could. The sixth years rolled their eyes, predicting what would come next.

"And why would you be correcting me?"

"Um what? I was just telling you how to pronounce my name," JW replied, his face blanching.

"If I required help I would have asked for it," she snapped. "I do not like an aggressive pupil in my class, now all you have to say was *here* you did not need to interrupt my register," she said hotly. Steam rose from her ears.

"I was not interrupting, merely telling you how to say a Dutch name, you said it wrong," he replied bluntly, trying to hold his own when every fibre of his body wanted to shrink back into his chair and disappear.

"I do believe I know how to pronounce names in all languages, now stop disrupting my class or I will have to ask you to leave. I propose you wouldn't want that, not on your first day, Mr Wow-ters."

"It's Vow-ters, you say the W as a V sound, please stop-!"

"Just call him JW, okay Miss Duvall?" the boy with the goatee hurriedly burst out with, his friend beside him shaking with a laughter he had to hold in. The teacher blushed profusely. The rest of the pupils glanced at each other nervously, some holding tightly to their desks for comfort out of fear, while others were biting their lips and trying not to laugh.

"Yes, okay, now I'll continue..." As she resumed marking the list of pupils present on her register the door popped open with a sheepishly showy clunk against the metal filing cabinet to its right.

"AH! Sorry we're late, we got separated from our buddy!"

"And who might you be?" Miss Duvall demanded, standing up and clenching her fists behind her back as she saw the face of two pale, freckled girls who had just burst into her classroom.

"Ally Jackson, friends call me AJ, and this quine is Mel- she's very shy- we both got lost you see cos we couldn't see our buddy in the canteen before the bell rang- I gi-,"

"ENOUGH!" interrupted the teacher.

"Um, rude much?" AJ harrumphed, motioning Melissa to come inside with her, and pushed her way into the classroom to sit at the back with Jordan and a ginger haired boy who sat two seats away.

"First warning," Miss Duvall sighed with exasperation. The S6 buddies allowed Melissa and AJ to pass by them to sit down.

"She sure talks a lot," JW whispered to Perry on the other side of the classroom.

"Ah yeah, she's a right Chatterbox, Connor let's call her that okay?" Perry said, swinging back in his chair to talk to a fellow member of their peer group and former pupil of Applegrove primary school, a boy who had found himself by the window next to the class goths- Aiden Peterson and Anna Pearson.

"WAIT, now that everyone is accounted for, and I'll put that on the register. And the first troublemakers have been realised; that's you two girls," She said writing on the board, and then she wrote Perry quickly allowing the boy to gasp, he made a loud gulp that made several girls giggle. "For swinging in your chair," she added.

Melissa had been in shock when Jade hadn't turned up to guide her to class. It was a further blow to find out that the loudest most talkative girl in her registration class was in fact a half-sister of their buddy. It was saddening to discover that her favourite sixth year had shirked her duties to go out for a cigarette between Mathematics and German. In turn she was not surprised when during the Birthday seating roulette she had been put directly in from of the teacher's desk. It was another disappointment to add to her first day.

"Oh good, we're next to the weirdo who was late," she heard Perry trying to whisper to the blonde in the seat next to her. She blushed profusely when JW turned his head and she realised through his sea-green eyes that he was in fact a boy. She blushed ever deeper when he gave her a cute half-smile and introduced himself in an accent she didn't recognise. JW in the meantime was reeling from just being told to cut his hair. It was an unavoidable comment because he had been stood next to Samantha, who was also born in July, during the seating line-up. Samantha, he thought, who had already told her friends about pulling his hair before registration. Successfully managed to emasculate him in their vicious whispers ever since- "He's such a princess," they had hissed- and he had tried to ignore it, but it made him feel paranoid.

"Did you hear he tried to dye it blonde himself?" a random girl asked a bit too loudly as they were lining up, and he knew they were gossiping about him. Samantha came and stood beside him and uttered the fateful words in a condescending tone.

"You know, if you don't want people to think you're a girl, you should cut it..." She had snarled; and after a girl he had just met and would have to sit next to and do group work with, for at least a whole term, OBVIOUSLY blushed with embarrassment over his hair, JW was now considering it.

While JW, Perry and Melissa had been forced to sit in a group of three in the front desk in front of the evil Miss Duvall, Jordan found himself in the back row of the seating plan, next to the goths. He saw Aiden and Anna who were gazing out of the window, looking forlornly at their previous seats, which was now occupied by the gang of Samantha and the other athletic popular girls. The oversized ginger of the class was the first one Jordan decided to speak to.

"Do you know any German or did you just choose this because French was full?"

"Kase, that means cheese," James Mitchell replied sharply.

"Cheese, I like cheese," Jordan replied in an affirmative tone as he sat down and hung his bag and coat on the back of the chair. He took out his plastic pencil case and they were handed out their class jotters for German by the two sixth year buddies. They wrote their names on the dark green German jotters, which had been handed out by the two sixth year young men, along with the class allocation code of 2F.

"...cheese," James repeated, nodding to his new companion.

"...cheese..." Jordan sighed, tilting his head back to watch James graffiti on his jotter a picture of a slice of cheese on a mouse trap. He tried to copy him but his slice was not as cool. Then they coloured in the drawings and swapped jotters to draw more cheese related things on each other's jotters. They did this until Miss Duvall noticed they hadn't been paying attention to her and demanded they open their jotters or get warnings. They slouched back and waited for the class to be over.

"Oh lordy, why did Jady have to miss all that?" AJ gasped laughing out gregariously as she made her way out of class holding onto Melissa's jumper by the shoulder. Melissa shrugged and let her classmate guide her through the crowd until they came to the end of the corridor. They had a few looks from other students as they came to the end of the corridor and turned to go towards the mathematics corridor. There was Jade, stood with the other students in sixth year who she hung out with, she had her back turned to them as they came up to her.

"Hey!" AJ hollered, launching herself onto the older girl.

"Woah, is this must be your sister we've heard so much about.

And hey, is this the one Edina mentioned?" Asked one of the sixth years, while pointing directly at Melissa.

"Melissa?" gasped a freckled girl who stood motionless outside of their little group. The freckled girl had mid-length straight auburn hair and her lips strained together in a thin line. For the first time that week, Melissa turned to see her best friend.

Chapter Two

You could tell it was a mathematics corridor by the Pythagoras triangles drawn on the walls. Higher up it screamed "SOH-CAH-TOA" and lower down it had drawings of triangles. It was painted mostly blue to match the linoleum, and the doors, and to explain the classrooms being number B9, B12 and so it went. Some of the décor was orange and green to differentiate. Bulletins were printed on white paper, tiny black type-face, and hung in straight lines along the walls at eye height with blue-tac or staples. It was shy knowledge but there were also three computer classrooms in the middle of the corridor, joined together through adjoining doors, with little square windows, and not shouted about because they were ashamed about the decrepit computers they contained. Louise Owens was thoroughly observant with her eyes as she was pushed through the corridor to join the queue with her privileged Brainiac classmates. She assumed that because of the placement of the classroom being the closest to the foyer and that would make them the first in all her peers to make it to the canteen, they were the superior of all the first years. She noted that many of her classmates were from the same primary school, Applegrove, which often taught the best mathematics curriculum, going on the peer group who joined her first year Mathematics class. Louise flipped her hair and said hello to the girl beside her, who smiled graciously in return and so they engaged in pompous small talk. It was there Louise saw her best friend and her face soured.

"Melissa?" she gasped, her body tensing up as she stood in the queue of children waiting outside Mr Murtagh's classroom. She felt her cheekbones flush red underneath her freckled face as she saw the group approaching. The sixth years and the blonde haired first year girls all smelling wretched. It was an assault to the nostrils of perfume and body spray that failed to cover the ickiest smell of all. Smoke. Louise fumed. She could not be affiliated with smokers. It was a disgusting habit.

"Hi!" Melissa called out quickly.

"Jordan, what?" Louise said after she spotted the short boy hiding behind the lanky copper haired boy with freckles on his round pale face. She barely managed to hide her disdain for him from her voice- glaring behind her hazel eyes at the girls.

"Louise..." Jordan mumbled through gritted teeth.

"Who's this Melissa? Friend of yours?" Jade spat out, sensing the chill in the air and in an effort to disperse the tension.

"And I'm James!" He laughed over the top of the sixth year, smiling brightly as he launched himself forward to shake hands with the long haired, red haired freckled girl who might as well have been his female twin if not for the difference in form and charisma. "Pleased tae mecha. What's the story here, eh?" He asked down towards his new friends. Melissa looked shyly at her feet and mumbled.

"We three are n-neigh-boors, and these two went out over the summer. They broke up yesterday," she shrugged and when she was asked to repeat louder Louise made a grumpy sigh.

"Melissa, Jordan, and I live in the same street. Melissa is *my best friend* and Jordan lives in the house between our two. *I dumped him,*" She blurted out. They received interested glances and raised eyebrows from surrounding classmates.

"Hey Baps!" catcalled a male student over the heads of the first year pupils- JW and Perry bringing up the rear from the language corridor hidden behind his back. Jade rolled her eyes and made eye contact with the skinny misogynist wearing a sixth year jumper and a flimsy goatee. Guy's like him were why girls like her were single- all those immature hormones and nicknames like that.

"Yeah, alright!" one of her friends called back. It was the lanky first year class-clown type that surprised her by spinning on his heels to face to face with his adversary.

"Would I be right in assuming that you call her that just because of her tits? Cheap talk coming from you, anyone ever say that you look like Stalin?" James replied. Challenging the older boy to stare him down. The girls in the older group stifled giggles while the first years were awed into silence by their comrade.

"Wow, tough talk. You better get to class, kid. Mrs Riddoch don't talk kindly to lateness from clowns like you. Being the head of the department and all," Goatee Stalin rebuked, reasserting authority, but also glancing nervously at his peers.

"Thanks James, but he's right about Mrs Riddoch," Jade gave a sigh of relief. "You guys better come down the end of the corridor to class, I'll show you the way. Then again, depends on how you act," she added, winking at her sister. She said goodbye to her friends and motioned for James, Melissa, AJ and Jordan to follow her to the classroom at the right end on the corner just before you turned towards the English corridor.

"Bye, Mel, see you after school!" Louise declared quickly, waving to her friend. Melissa smiled and waved back in agreement.

The first years were herded into their different classrooms and Louise did her best to give a fake smile as she was directed into a seat via random selection by their teacher. She exchanged polite introductions with her four new companions who she would make sure to befriend during the next few weeks. They all sat in their little grey table and wobbly chairs, pencil cases out, waiting for their new jotters to be delivered and politely thanking the classroom assistant... A pale flat-chested sixth year student with an unfortunate brown bob and oval shaped pink spectacles- who blushed when she walked away from Louise. This is the one thing that made Louise feel self-conscious in the entire world. Over the summer she had blossomed into an AA cup which did not fit under her old school shirt. Her mother had bought the shirt before they had been forced to rush out onto a dreadfully awkward mother-daughter trip to buy her first bra.

"Welcome everyone, first we are going to start with a short quiz, a couple of mental arithmetic questions so I can guess where all of your strengths and weaknesses are. Then. When the text books arrive, as they have been delayed in the post, I will direct you through section one of the book which is geometry, and by the time we finish this we'll be moving onto section two which will be basic algebra. This should take us up to the October holidays. Any questions?"

"What do the textbooks look like?" Asked a girl near the teacher's desk and he displayed a dog-eared copy of the red S1 textbooks with a photo of the fancy column in Edinburgh, the teacher talked about the beautiful architecture they used on the range of textbooks but it was of no interest to her "I can see why they had to order new books for us, give the ones with graffiti and missing pages to the dumb kids," Louise whispered to the girl on her left who muttered in agreement, smiling politely. Louise paid attention in class as she did in all of her classes during the day. Lunch she waited in the queues with her classmates as she got to know them on her first day quickly determining who the right person to get close to was and who she needed to keep at a distance. Following lunch she had two more classes before making her way through the throngs of students to meet Melissa outside. She shouted after her friend and they walked together along the pavement. Amicable silence until they dawdled to the end of Burdshaugh road.

"Oh look it's my cousin, David!" She declared spontaneously. The small boy skid to a stop on the curb beside the two eleven year olds, his bike breaks making a loud jarring squeal.

"Hey girls!" he gasped, giggling as he settled his bike between his legs so that both wheels and his tiptoes were on the ground- he had to stretch just a little as his bike was a bit big for him just now- he would grow into it soon enough. "I guess I'll walk with you two."

*

A few days later Louise and Melissa were walking home from school when they were speaking about a task set by their separate English teachers. Louise began the conversation.

"I've realised it's not much difference to Applegrove, aside from there being a mix of kids from other schools in the area,

43

including Dyke, Kinloss and whatever else there is! I'm more than a little surprised that I get on well with some of them, so that's write I wrote to my P7! What about you?" She asked her friend, shrugging her bag on her shoulder as they walked.

"Err, well, I wrote about how the primary school visits and tours before the holidays made the school seem really nice."

"And? That sounds really boring if you're just going to say that!" Louise interjected, rolling her eyes.

"I also wrote that I hadn't expected to be so scared on the first day..." Melissa mumbled quickly, blushing and dipping her face to hide behind her fringe as they ambled along the path in front of the river.

"I also wrote about the buddies, cos my teacher said they'd want to hear about that, I suppose you wrote about that Jade girl," Louise scoffed, not even bothering to hide her disgust, she scowled as her name curled around the last words.

"Um, well, actually... I wrote about how my buddy was really nice and that made Mrs Brown want to read it out in front of class, I was really embarrassed, cos-," Melissa began but was rudely interrupted by her best friend.

"Oh well she must have been impressed, and how did that fair with the rest of your class?"

"Ah, it forced Jade to blush when she heard about it. She called me a *wee star* and she gave me such a big hug I almost drowned."

"Jordan was jealous of that I bet," Louise added.

"Yeah, so then her sixth year friends loved me for that, they even said they'd like me to hang out with them sometimes."

"What?" gasped Louise, her eyebrows twitching and her face beginning to boil a lobster red. The group from Jade's gang welcoming Melissa as they had done with AJ; that was just not on! Infuriated, Louise quickly changed the subject to something she liked better.

"I made friends with a couple girls in my Drama class and there's one or two boys that are interested in me. They always ask that I be in their groups for the tasks. During one lesson I was the star of my own little tableau," Louise gushed, passionately. "It was like a scene where there was two boys fanning me with pretend giant leaves and one of them pretending to feed me grapes. It was so much fun, you should have been there to see me!"

"Yeah, talking about boys Jordan and this guy called JW are getting along well. They were talking about hanging out one weekend, to play Zelda, but I told them you'd still not like me to hang out with Jordan."

"Good, thank you. Mel, that's why you're my best friend!"

"Oh yeah, of course," Melissa replied automatically, blushing.

"Wait, hang on, you've mentioned JW every time we've talked this week... you've got a crush, haven't you?" Louise interjected quizzically, putting both her hands out dramatically to stop her friend mid-step. She held her friend's wrists gently, the shorter Melissa blushing intently and trying to avoid eye contact.

"No, no, no, no! I's-I mean- He's friends with Jordan and Perry! They're horrible and tease me during classes. I haven't had a crush since primary six," Melissa replied quickly, her words tripping over themselves.

"Well, okay, if you don't have a crush on him tell me what he wrote in his P7 letter? Be honest, I can tell if you're lying," Louise demanded, holding eye contact.

"JW wrote about how he liked his new friends but missed his old friends who were not able to go to the academy yet..." Melissa mumbled quietly in reply, squirming and fidgeting, her eyes darting from her friends face to her feet and hands.

"Go on," Louise urged, smiling excitedly.

"JW felt that still people had trouble with his accent and wrote that not very much for him had been different to how he had expected..." Melissa added.

"Hmm, yeah I hear that, but this doesn't convince me you don't have a crush, not at all."

"Bu-but, Jordan and James copied each other in what they wrote and got an annoyed lecture from the teacher- who then laughed at them and said that they had been the best results of the transition from primary school because of how they had used teamwork to get the letter done. So I'm not like giving JW extra special attention!" Melissa interrupted quickly, her friend sighed and let go of her.

"Right..." Louise said, rolling her eyes. They walked the rest of the way home without talking about JW, or any other boys, again and Melissa made an extra effort to avoid talking about him to her best friend.

The first weeks of first year went by without incident, until...

Chapter Three

As Melissa gazed out of her bedroom window she could just about see two boys playing in the park across the street. One was dark haired and skinny while the other had copper blonde hair, cropped close to his head, and looked slightly taller. They were both a little naturally tanned, although one more olive complexioned than the other. She bit her lip and considered the boys might have been Jordan and his older brother Max, but then Max was especially pale and blonde, then she exhaled sharply and turned away from the window, covering her blushing face in her hands. The other boy was JW. She tried to compose herself by laughing it off.

"Mel, you want to tell me what happened in school this week?" Her best friend said, curiously, from her perch on the bed. Louise had her legs tucked under herself, posing like a model for a photoshoot in her mature nightgown over her nightdress that they had worn for their sleepover. Melissa was dressed comfortably in her own pyjamas, which were just an old t-shirt and matching bottoms. On the bedside table there was an assortment of junk food. Sweets, chocolate, juice and crisps spread out in plastic containers. Neatly arranged by Louise and both the girls had carried them upstairs- now they were all soft from being left out overnight but still edible. Melissa grabbed a handful of crisps and sat on the bed with her friend.

"Ok, just promise don't tell Kirsty, or I'll be mad," she insisted.

"I swear, I'm your secret keeper, I couldn't tell her if you make me pinkie-promise on it, and anyway she's away to *Craig's* for the Tatty hols."

"Okay, let's do that," Melissa said nodding, she laced pinkies with her friend and ate with her free hand. Louise took some as well before Melissa started to set the scene.

*

In school throughout the first term JW felt as if he was put into situations where he was forced to talk to Melissa. They were given group tasks in German, Geography, English and Drama every week together. He tried to make an effort to get along with her but there was something he genuinely found unnerving about her. He made this clear in his body language and it had a harmful impact on Melissa, whom was also trying to act normal despite what some said about her. She was aware that JW got bullied as well on the times she went to lunch up the high street with classmates.

"So why is your voice funny?" people asked him, and he would explain that he was from the Netherlands.

"Neverland? Like Peter Pan?" A boy in class said laughing! Melissa tended to just listen when she heard exchanges like that one. There was a few times when it lead to more than just JW shrugging it off. Sometimes he became enraged about being called Peter Pan. Especially when James tried to stick up for his new friend.

"Don't listen to him J, he's just a numpty," the redhead said, smirking and trying to make light of the situation.

49

"Who are you calling a numpty?" was the angered eleven year olds reply. His actions and name calling always lead to a shoving match between all of the first year boys in their F class. Melissa and the girls in their class rarely found it interesting after the first few times it had happened- during the times they were waiting to get into class usually, especially before Music when Alana's friends had just had some "fresh-air" and the smell of smoke got on the nerves of the non-smokers. It was a certain class divide- in more ways than one.

"Just stay away from each other if you can't wait outside class sensibly," the music teacher ordered, making sure to put Perry's group with Jordan and the boys on different sides of the classroom from the more boisterous boys.

"Everyone knows music class is a skive anyway," Alana whispered to Melissa...

*

"Ugh you're still friends with her? Please tell me your story gets more interesting, come on! Enough context! I know your timetable as well as my own!" Louise thundered, interrupting Melissa's flashback.

"Ok, I'll just move onto the thing that happened."

"Yes please!" Louise exclaimed, clasping her hands together and making her eyes like a puppies. "Sorry for interrupting, please just get to the good stuff!"

*

Mrs Bright sat quietly at her desk with an eye on the door as she waited for all of the first year pupils to filter in. As they hung up their bags, jackets and coats, and as they sat down in the circle of chairs in the middle of the drama classroom she mentally prepared herself for the lesson ahead.

"Good morning everyone, please take your seats. Now, today we're going to start by warming up with a game to get everyone up and moving into seats that are more randomized." Mrs Bright declared, her stifling a heavy sigh as she pushed herself up. She adjusted her half-moon spectacles and stood aside from behind the desk to present to the class. The knots of her poncho that masked her curved frame swayed as she moved. Melissa sat in a spot close to the back corner of the room, the nearest classmates to her were two seats away until someone was forced, with obvious hesitation, to sit beside her. After weeks of this behaviour Melissa had stopped taking it to heart- she was excited to play a game that would make people move seats to places they weren't allowed to choose. Mrs Bright floated around the circle allocating everyone a fruit for the game before the room became a flurry of excitement when she started to shout commands.

"Apple! Orange! Pear! Fruit salad!" was how it sounded. Quickly Melissa and her peers swapped seats until the scramble when the teacher shouted out the last one. Everyone was trying their best but some collided and stepped on each other in the mad rush.

"Orange!" the teacher shouted, and Melissa watched Jordan and Perry stand up before she moved to the nearest spot where they had vacated. It went on like this for about five minutes. Melissa could feel the blood pumping the last time she sat down when she heard others panting and saw some red faces. They laughed because it was fun but gave a unanimous sigh when the teacher said; "Oh no, this won't do, boy-girl order please!"

"Oh come on!" a boy named Aiden grumbled as he was asked to swap places with Angela to sit between two girls, leaving his friends behind. Angela, simply smiled and with a little effort, moved to sit between James and Ross. Aiden sulked in a gothic contrast. Melissa found herself sat beside JW.

"Oh hello," he said to her as he sat down, but he didn't look at her, it was as if he was speaking to someone on the far side of the room.

"Hi-hi!" she remembered to say quickly, injecting a cheery upbeat tone despite feeling a little out of breath from the running around they had just been doing.

"Ok, now that we are seated appropriately I would like you all to stand up," Mrs Bright said raising her hands up to symbolise the rising up.

"This is so lame," Jordan mumbled getting up.

"Relax Jord, it's not that far for you to go," another boy said attempting a joke. "Cos he's short," he then added, yet still no one laughed.

"I want you to take this rose and pass it to the person to your left saying "this is for you" and then they must say "thank you" and then repeat to the next person, and so on, but do it in the most theatrical way possible. The one whom I judge to be the best at this activity gets to keep the rose," Ms Bright announced to the class producing a red and green long-stemmed plastic rose from her top desk drawer. She demonstrated by handing the rose to the first student with an awe-like expression and saying "this is for you" as if she was bestowing a token to the blushing prince, who for his credit tried not to mumble as he said his thanks before repeating the line to the girl on his left. The class participated in the exercise with reluctant enthusiasm, passing the rose around, different person to person displaying how much their bashfulness and confidence was clashing. Melissa prepared herself mentally as she watched her classmates perform.

"Perry, this is for you," Jenny said, looking as if the rose was cursed she held it out to him at arm's length with a stricken look on her face. Perry bowed thoughtfully as he accepted the rose and then prepared to toss it to Samantha quietly, he acted as if he was confident yet there was an obvious nervous shake when he repeated the act towards Steph, the tallest and blondest girl in their class- with whom he was rumoured to have a crush on- and she then curtsied like a princess in her acceptance. Perry looked down when the classes' attention was removed from him.

"Thank you" and "This is for you" repeated in total of eighteen times before it made its way over to Melissa. Jordan pretended it was a grenade as he tossed the rose to Alisha, who then gracefully handed it over to James, who produced it with a flourish from her hand, giving the back of her hand a soft kiss. She giggled and blushed and then the class was still laughing as James went down on bended knee to hand the rose to Melissa...

*

"What?" Louise interrupted. "Oh, that ginger guy!"

"Of course James made everyone laugh, he actually got down on one knee and said 'this is for you' like a proposal! I got so red in the face it was all I could do to utter the words 'Thank you' and then 'this is for you' to the next person... but the next person was JW," Melissa explained to her friend who rolled her eyes.

"This is for you," Melissa said, handing the rose to JW. Handing it to him as if she was going to give him a handshake, accidentally brushing her palm against his. The first time she touched his hands. There was a fraction of static in the air between them before she let go of the rose. Then she heard him say her name as she fell back onto the hard floor.

Melissa recalled what she could of the third-hand version of events, as she had been told them, but for the benefit of Louise she kept things brief.

"What's happened, I think she's fainted!" JW gasped with a mixture of shock, nervousness and confusion laced through his voice.

"Keep calm everyone, Melissa, are you awake?" This fainting causes a couple of things to happen; Mrs Bright has to keep her first years calm and decide whether to call the nurse or request an ambulance.

"Oh! My! Goodness!" Steph and some of her friends squealed backing away, they muttered that JW had hit Melissa and were panicking in the corner. The other pupils panic and start to accuse Melissa of being overly dramatic, make fun of her for passing out. All the while JW is panicky because he was standing right beside Melissa when she fainted and he's self-conscious about how he looks from the events as they or accused JW of hurting her.

"You need to call an ambulance, Mrs Bright!" Jenny said, blushing red. Some of the boys were laughing on the corner by the door.

"Tell them it's not funny," Samantha added, and with that turned away to confront the boys, stomping over to them.

"Calm down everyone, please!" Mrs Bright said again, waving her arms in the air gesturing for them to lower their volume.

"What's happened?" came the concerned voice of Miss Cox from the doorway. Some students out in the hall gawping like seagulls tried to peek past her to see what the commotion was about.

"Go get the nurse please, Jordan?"

"Hell, James come with me!" Jordan ordered, his face ashen. James and Jordan, as well as a few girls wish to express concern for Melissa– Angela, Alisha and Kirsten leaning over her in a circle on the floor, next to JW who hastened to agree with them- muttering her name and swearing under his breathe.

"No need to swear, she'll be alright," Miss Cox shrilled. Perry and the popular crew were panicky, want to start gossiping immediately sort of thing, make a big deal about it and speculation- JW wanted to impress them too but he knew they would blame him for this incident.

Meanwhile Melissa is lying on the rock hard floor, her consciousness far away in a dreamlike suspension of time: She could see flashes of pictures. Him kissing her but she could not believe what she was seeing. JW waving on the edge of her mind like a ghost.

She had heard him saying her name but it felt far away. A hoarse raspy voice but it was definitely his. It felt so real. It felt like her eyelids were covered by a black sheet and someone else was stabbing it with an invisible needle, allowing pinpricks of white light through until the black sheet was completely dissolved and she was staring at the big gaping whiteness. All she could hear after that were the shouting of her classmates before she lost consciousness completely. She was certain that at some point a PE teacher had carried her to the disabled elevator because the next thing had had happened was she had then woken up in the school nurse's office which was located upstairs. She sat on the rock-hard patient observation bed, alone, in front of her Dad. She dared not to tell Louise about that part though.

Chapter Four
Steiner school, Cluny Hill

It was a cool September afternoon. Melinda played with her friends outside of the Steiner school, as she did every day before getting the bus home. The rope tied to the tire suspended from a large strong tree sending her spiralling through the air. Adrenaline and physics rocketing her forward. The wind and dirt in her hair as she hangs onto the rope with all her might. She's giggling with a youthful childlike glee, and it is a beautiful picture, spoiled only by the four boys that separated us. I smile.

"Woo Hoo!" She shouts with excitement.

"Do you ever feel like you're being watched?" A boy leaning against the tree asked towards her and the others. I feel a pang of jealousy towards him as she snaps her head back in his direction. This is the musical enthusiast who she has adored for the last term. Dean! I think to myself with stymied anger, clenching my fists but doing my best to keep myself quiet as a mouse, to remain invisible.

"Don't be daft, Dean, you toadstool," spoke the blonde haired boy with the Swedish accent. I can't be bothered to remember his name. Jacob? Yannick? "Hamiz, it's your turn," he called out to the short ruddy boy who was a couple years below them in the Steiner school. English was third language to him so he was almost mute. He struggled with it like most things but they included him. Most boys would have been outcast and ridiculed for this kind of behaviour, but in their special school bullying was almost non-existent.

"When is the bus again? I want to get some delicious blueberry Slush Puppies!" Melinda declares with ecstatic passion. I gaze at her lugubriously; if only she could think of me in the same way as she does those ice cold sweet drinks.

"We can do this for another half hour before we should head down the hill, big sis," the Swede replied, patting her on the head as she skipped over to him. Dean was getting ready to push the mute boy on the tire swing. He has a strong arm, that's for sure. The swing flies out from the platform with a loud whoosh. Melinda cheers on her younger friend. After a couple minutes go by I make my way down the hill ahead of them so I can get into my car before they can dawdle down to the garage where they planned to purchase their beverages. From my 98' Golf I could see their group walking away from the garage. Melinda matching stride with the boys with her long legs. Linked arms with Hamiz and, Dean. I struggled not to snarl as I watch them skip along, not a care in the world...

I watched them after school the next day as well. It was a Wednesday, so Melinda was staying in Forres until later in order to go to her trampoline group. She attended with 10 other young girls from the area. Her guy friends from the Steiner School sometimes came to watch her through big glass spectating windows at the community centre before they got the bus to their different homes. Dean lived at Findhorn, I knew this from monitoring him. The others were less important.

"Steiner School!" A group of teenage boys called out towards Melinda and her friends, chanting it and laughing. The gang from the Academy with short gelled back hair, cigarettes and varying degrees of unwashed aromas emitting from their ragged, low riding jeans and Adidas sweaters. One of the boys was over 6 feet tall and wore bright yellow boxers covered in smiley faces. Could not be unseen. I rolled my eyes at their cheeky behaviour, watching them from my alleyway hiding space, listening patiently for the response.

"Forres Academy!" Melinda's friends shouted back with their louder enthusiasm. The Academy boys blushed, grumbling in defeat, and sulked away to nurse their egos. They continued to walk towards the community centre laughing and ignoring the gang of chavs. Laughing. Until they saw another group of teens from the Academy, but it was someone whom spoke to them with a little more respectful demeanour.

"Dean!" the boy with long blonde hair exclaimed, he looked to be about eleven or twelve, going from the pitch of his voice and height. His face was slightly tanned just like Dean's, I could see him from this angle, but I could barely make out his facial features. "I haven't seen you in ages!" he added, and immediately from his voice I could tell he was either American or Dutch.

"Oh, little man, how are you doing?" Dean enquired passionately, and they spoke as if they were old friends. Melinda did not add much to the conversation, being strangers, but when asked why and what they were doing that evening she answered politely.

"I'm going to gymnastics, these guys were just walking me. They're probably going to hangout in the community centre too," she added with a shrug. In my experience it was suspicious of me to be seen watching her group at gymnastics so I took my leave then. As painfully jealous as I was that she would now have yet more foreign looking boyfriends joining her. I sulked to my car and drove home in the fading September sun, accompanied by Beethoven and Radio Alba on my car stereo to lift my spirits.

Chapter Five

The thing that happens of importance is that Melissa "faints" in drama class after being made to touch JW's hand by accident through a group activity... and now

Louise gobbled down a couple cola bottles from a bag that they had located in the kitchen and they sat in the living room. Melissa's Dad was on his computer ignoring both the girls to code. The television was on to something random as background noise.

"So you saw a thing?"

"Yeah, I mean..." Melissa mumbled inherently, sighing.

"What?" Louise scoffed, "Pretty lame, sounds like just a typical day dream," she said dismissing the premonition completely and refusing to acknowledge it as more than a simple day dream of a crush. *Melissa totally fancies him,* Louise thought to herself, *she's just too afraid to admit it, but she talks about him all the time and now she's seeing visions of him.* She imagined what JW might look like and expected to be disappointed. She was so done with first year boys.

"What does?!" Richard asked, curiously, his body slightly turned towards the couch, an eye on the television set.

"Nothing!!" the two girls shouted, embarrassed, giggling awkwardly. They glanced at each other, wondering and waiting patiently for what he was going to say next, anticipating conversation.

"Okay, now, don't I remember you two saying that you were actually going to go out? You know I saw Jordan go out to the park, why don't you go see how he's doing?" Richard suggested, eager to get peace to watch something more interesting – like a documentary on the History channel. Louise rolled her eyes and uncrossed her legs. Melissa shuffled off the couch to sit on the edge, she joined her after another eye roll, because Jordan.

"Dad, we were about to, just wanted to check if there was anything to record for later. Promise you'll make sure it does that?" Melissa requested, standing up straight and grabbing the remote.

"Yes, of course," Her Dad replied immediately pivoting back to face his computer screen. The two girls prepared themselves, collecting all of their junk food wrappers, agreeing to leave the rest of the snacks behind for Richard.

It was a warm autumn day, the trees that lined the street and park area were just beginning to lose their colour. The girls chose to wear fleece jackets with their trousers and trainers. It was chilly in the shade, Louise claimed, as they crossed the empty road to go to the park. They moseyed along the path and when they entered through the gate, there Jordan and a friend were having a dashing sword fight. Straight sharp sticks broken off from the nearby trees were their weapons of choice and they made perfect fencing swords.

"H-hi!" Melissa gasped, rocking on the gate as she entered the park. She could barely catch her breath nor contain her excitement. There was a massive rush at seeing JW outside school. Louise squinted and smiled warmly.

"Oh, hello, I'm Louise," She exclaimed barging into the middle of the sword fight, a stick glancing off of hair. "Jordan! I swear you did that on purpose," she snapped, her face rapidly pink and looking as if steam might escape her ears.

"It was not!" Jordan grumbled obediently.

"H-hi," JW interjected, flipping down his sword swiftly so that he didn't get the same treatment. His eyes curiously wide as Louise came over to stand directly in front of him. She curtsied and introduced herself again. He squeaked a reply.

"Don't be scared of her, this is just how she is," Jordan admitted cheerily, throwing down his weapon with a shrug. Louise growled and stalked over to stand beside Melissa near the park gate.

"He's kind of cute," she whispered to her with a hand cupped around her mouth so that only she could hear. The two girls both giggled and the boys watched with intrigue.

"Is it okay if we carry on? We were right in the middle of something, but you girls can watch," Jordan enquired, giving a side glance towards his friend. The blonde raised an eyebrow in return and shrugged.

"Sure thing," Louise replied without hesitation. Melissa blushed. The boys laughed into a show stopping sword fight. They also seemed to be pretending to be pirates which Louise rolled her eyes at. Melissa thought it was cool. She could just picture JW dressed as a dashing hero, paring with Jordan and catching his sword with every move. Jordan was more like Captain Hook or Long John Silver. He fought with one hand and had his other hand in a constant hook shape with his finger. The two boys fought and parried, their sticks bouncing and glancing off each other causing the wood to creak and the bark split off in all directions.

"You can't deny it anymore, Captain Jack!" Jordan shouted rashly, panting slightly. "You're getting tired and that drink doesn't help your balance!"

"Nae, says I!" JW barked back, and adopted a swagger and swayed a little, pretending to be drunk on his feet as he wobbled, yet his body maintained a fluid motion as he danced about. Jordan eventually managed to back JW into the corner where it looked like he might win, when a bright idea fell over JW's face and he looked down in surprise. "You're going to give up first, Long John!" he spat, knocking Jordan back and dealing him a loud tap across the shin that would no doubt leave him bruised.

"No, my peg leg!" Jordan grimaced, grabbing his foot and pulling it back with his spare hand - the other holding the stick. The girls giggled as they watched Jordan hop about on one leg.

"Let's see you best me when you have to hop about!"

"Och, a'rite, I concede!" Jordan grumbled when his stick was broken in two after a couple of difficult seconds. He flopped onto the park bench. "Next time you can be the cripple and I'll be Captain Jack, cos that always gives the advantage..." Jordan mumbled throwing away his stick. He rolled up his trouser leg and stretched his leg out on the bench and examined it. JW mumbled an apology but his friend claimed it as a part of the game. Both boys smiled and turned towards the girls who had pretended to talk among themselves.

"Well, let's see how you two handle it, shall we?" JW asked, spinning his stick around in a circle. Melissa turned slightly and looked up into his face as walked over, spinning the wooden play sword, he gave a coy half smile. His eyes met hers and he dropped the stick mid spin. Melissa blushed as she felt it whack against her thigh.

"Woah! Do that again!" Jordan gasped, his cheeks red and his mouth agape. JW did so. Melissa felt the reverberation from her backside as it travelled through her nerves.

"You mischievous devil!" Melissa hissed, the look he gave her was teasing. She sighed and crossed her arms.

"Cool, can I try?" Jordan asked and Melissa went scarlet as she felt another light whack.

"Your bum jiggles like a bowl full of jelly," Louise realised, not even bothering to hold back her enjoyment at her best friend's embarrassment.

"Please stop," she whimpered, confused how she should feel that JW was smacking her behind. She was a little excited by the attention but also completely mortified.

"Come on, Mel, it's just a bit of harmless fun!" Jordan added, reaching for the stick. JW held it high above his reach and Louise yanked it from him.

"Ok, we're taking this now, Jordan is not allowed to spank anyone around here," Louise declared, holding it close to her waist. JW raised an eyebrow and shared a look with the other boy.

"Would you be jealous?" the Dutch boy asked, curiously, with a now mischievous grin, he looked down at the tight jeans she was wearing. "Because if you want I could see how jelly-like yours is too," he grinned and held out his open palm. His friend sniggered, rocking back on his heels, and enjoying watching his ex-girlfriend squirm.

66

"I just mean, that you've had enough of torturing poor Mel," she hastened to add, blushing slightly as she covered the back of her jeans with her hands so the stick lay between her legs like a tail.

"R-right," JW assured her, winking at Melissa who was already sweating from the embarrassment of him playing with her curves and couldn't think straight to even talk. Her heart was going a mile a minute and her stomach felt as if it was full of butterflies. Louise looked at her and her heart bled; Melissa looked so besotted and breathless, it was too much.

"I think it's time we went back inside, people to see and all that," Louise excused, doing her best to shove Melissa out of the park.

"Oh, but you girls just got here," Jordan pouted, grabbing onto Mel's arm.

"Nae, say I!" Melissa finally managed to say, brushing his arm away and shooting from the park. The butterflies were doing jumping jacks and her heart felt as if it was at her eyebrows when the two girls made it to the house.

"My, girl, what made you want to leg it?"

"JW kept looking at my fat tushie!" Melissa wheezed, her full head and neck completely flushed. The two girls sat on the front step.

"I'm sorry, that was just too adorable, next time I'll make him stop sooner; though, you looked like you were enjoying it."

"He smacked my fat butt," she added, and then was came over with a girlish giggle, "he spanked my butt," she repeated in different variations, consumed with a laugh that kept going until all the butterflies had flown and her ribs hurt instead.

"Yes, and it's a nice butt he has too," Louise whispered, her arm around Melissa, and her friend agreed with extra enthusiasm. They both sat on the porch giggling.

*

When school resumed from the October break Melissa had to hide from JW out of embarrassment. In fact, aside from speaking to her buddy and classmates the only person who she spoke to daily was her best friend- and that was mainly either before or after school. This meant she became invisible during break and lunch times. Melissa grew accustomed to drawing in her notebook on the small hill outside of the school. Occasionally, it did not feel so lonely...

"Mel! Mel!" AJ shouted, running towards her one day. The poor girl brought a stream of smoke and her posse behind her. She stopped in front of the girl who was sat on the grass. AJ smoked a lot, for a first year, so she hacked a cough and wheezed heavily.

"Your sister know you stole her *fags* again?" Melissa enquired almost in a whisper, putting emphasis on the word she most disliked using. She looked up at the strawberry blonde and was met by a sheepish grin. Ally nodded but hung her head back and dropped onto the grass- between coughing she muttered about Melissa being a "swot". The group plonked down around Melissa and it felt like a peaceful lunchtime, spent watching people, cars, birds and pupils. Her nose wrinkled. It irked her that the group of smokers followed her around but she was too nice to tell them to go away. She had one friend who knew how to.

"Melissa!!" Louise fumed, stomping over from the car park. She might as well have been fifty foot tall and towering over all the school minibuses and teacher's cars to get there. Her presents was ginormous as her manic aura consumed the group.

"Woah, calm the fuck down!" one of the older boys in their group said out loud, he craned his neck to look at the younger girl, he whistled. "Hey gorgeous, nice baps," he added, quickly changing his expression to a charming grin.

Louise pouted in chagrin and crossed her arm over her nearly developed bosoms. She relaxed her face but spoke through gritted teeth.

"Melissa, we spoke about this," was all that could be said.

"Sorry," the small girl whimpered in reply, collecting her things and rising up.

"Och this is ridiculous! Melly likes to spend time with me cos we're in class together and she's tight with my big sis. You can't just come up here and demand her to stop hanging out with us," AJ responded, jumping up onto her feet. She was an inch taller than Louise but on the incline she appeared taller. The alpha and beta wolves growled at each other, and the boys on the grass grew excited.

"It's a girl fight?" one whispered, "Bitch fight," was his replied hiss, correcting him.

"We're not going to fight," AJ sighed, crossing her arms to mirror Louise. Both the blonde girls who were standing on their toes rolled their eyes before they resumed glaring at each other. The electricity in the air grew static. "I think it's Melly's decision if she wants to hang with us. What do you say?"

"Okay, yeah," Louise admitted, lowering her arms in defeat.

"Um-um, ok," Melissa muttered, stuttering as the entire group turned towards her with wide eyes and expectant faces.

"Whatever you say, Mel, I'll respect. I'll be disappointed, but I promise you I will understand, so it's ok. We're cool," Ally Jackson raised, maturely.

"I-I, well, I know you guys all like to smoke, and I get that, but I don't really enjoy going around school smelling like *I smoke* because it gives *certain* people the wrong idea," she confessed, blushing.

"It's cool," AJ replied with a wink.

"I'm super *sorry,*" Melissa added, twiddling her hands.

She hugged the strawberry blonde girl briefly, which visibly irritated Louise, before saying goodbye to the group and waving as she strode down the hill. Louise gave one last glare to the gang before she turned. *I don't trust you,* she thought, her eyes meeting AJ's one last time. AJ smiled, her dark eyebrows meeting in a stark v shape. The group laughed and joked seconds later, which left Louise feeling paranoid.

Chapter Six

"Now, now settle down girls and boys, I'll get to you one by one over today and tomorrow," Mrs Elliott announced as all of her small class tried to clamber over her desk to get her to sign their forms. It was an odd sight for most teachers that a group of pupils would be so eager to get their parents an appointment with their Guidance teacher. As the head of Altair house, the blue school house and often known as the A-team in school Sports Days, *Mrs E* (as she was fondly called by the fifth and sixth years) was considered the best teacher overall. She was kind, considerate, encouraging, and could speak to all of the students. Her trick was to treat them as equals. More to the point the pupils liked her, she gave them good reviews and treats, and as a result of that all the parents wanted to meet her.

"Always the way, eh, Mrs E?" Jade said as she marched into the classroom and stood beside Melissa at the back of the queue.

Melissa looked up as the sixth year brushed against her arm and exhaled lightly. She glanced over, clutching her parent-teacher night timesheet that was lined with the evening timeslots available and a second side where Richard Galloway had written the teachers he wished to have a short interview with about his daughter's

71

progress. He wanted to see just about every teacher over the course of parent's night. Most of all Melissa wanted him to meet them. It was against her better judgement but she was eager to show him how well she was getting on in first year.

"Hey Mel, no hard feelings, we're still pals," Jade whispered to her after a beat. Melissa smiled and met eye contact with her teacher who returned her smile before continuing her chat with the pupil she was busy booking a timeslot for.

*

The bell rang for Anderson's primary for lunchtime on afternoon. The great crumbling building had been built as a high school over a hundred years ago, in the heart of Forres at the end of the main high street. The canteen and other school buildings were housed across the road was where the Forres Community House stands in the present day. In a sort of gimmick the school still separated boys and girls before entry, by having all the children line up in the archways in the playground before school. They had boys on the open left hand-side of the building and girls on the slightly narrower right. The boys were allowed a view of the Grant Park and Sunken Gardens, while the girls were wedged in next to the wall that separated their playground from the Butchers shop. An ancient joke of Forres town centre: Sweeney's Barbers is next door to the Butchers. There's also other commodities near to Andersons' Primary School, a chip shop, an ice cream shop and a sweetshop. It was the best for school lunchtimes during the school day because Forres Academy students were allowed to go up the high street, sit in the benches next to the

72

school railings and share their food with the peckish children. Children were always gripping up the railings, climbing and lollygagging with the older generation. However, not all Forres Academy kids were so generous. For a start there was Perry who snarled at the requests to share his lunch.

"Get away, feckin' seagulls," he moaned, "Get yer mammy's to buy your own bloody chips!" he said between mouthfuls. The girls called him names and then giggled when he had trouble with his food. He coughed so hard that passers-by gave him a concerned glance before they carried on walking, tut-tutting to themselves.

"Didn't your Mummy ever teach you to chew with *your* mouth closed?" a small girl about half his height retorted, probably only a few years younger than him. Perry blushed and turned away.

"Come on JW, let's go somewhere else," Perry grumbled, standing up from the bench. His friend followed obediently.

"That's right! Posh boy," The children in the navy blue uniforms sniggered, losing interest in him as he moved away from the benches towards the pavement.

"Jofeceal! Joso-fosy! Josephine!" Dean chirped in a sing-song voice as he approached the two eleven year olds with his posse while crossing the road. JW blushed, he just wanted to eat his chips, yet here's people disturbing him constantly. He tried to smile and greeted the older teenager.

"He calls you nicknames-like-that?" Perry screwed up his face as they came across the older boy and his friends. This one school lunchtime was turning into quite an irritation to him.

JW ducked his head down.

"That's so lame," he added, nudging his friend who could plainly tell from his expression was excited about seeing his guitar instructor- when he was also self-conscious about showing it.

"Not now Dean," JW mumbled, and received a rough ruffle of his hair in return.

"Not now Dean, JW is embarrassed because you go to the Steiner school," Perry corrected him. "You're uncool for him to be around, right now, see. He'll get bullied if people from the Academy spot him talking to your lot," He explained, feeling awkward. Dean looked down at Perry's shorts and bleach white legs.

"Me? *Uncool?* Not that it matters but I don't think I need to worry about that. In my school we might not follow the fads, we dress differently because there's no uniform, and despite all that bullying is almost non existent.

"As far as I can see the *uncool* one is you, but hey, I didn't start all this. I don't mind sticking to *my lot* because they have mutual understanding and respect for me. And I bet that even though you get good grades, you turned off from the conversation as soon as I started talking. I know about you, Perry, you think you're entitled because you receive praise and adoration, as a result of the training and talent for swimming real good. Hey-ho, don't listen to me, after all listening to an older person only shows respect, which I know you don't have."

"What did you say, sorry?" Perry muttered, focusing away towards a spot in the far distance.

74

"If it's what JW wants I won't speak to him, aside from during the lessons which his Mum pays for, cos she's cool and respects my teaching abilities."

"O-okay," JW managed to stutter out, hanging his head and looking down at his feet. He didn't want to admit he hated the thought of losing Dean as a friend but partly knew it was better to avoid the possibility of being picked on further.

"See you at five," Dean declared, and turned on his feet in the opposite direction.

Melissa noticed the only teachers who didn't call her shy in classes were the lessons she had with the Registration class. Johanna, Alisha, Gemma and all importantly Jade were excellent at helping her to feel included. She was also surprised in the report by her Religious Education teacher claimed she was unexpectedly outspoken, well read and intelligent on the subjects covered. This was a pleasing thing for her father to hear, although he was disappointed with her for doing so poorly in Mathematics and IT. On top of that she had glowing reviews from the Home Economics and Art teachers. In her S1 class she was so nervous because of the incidents that sometimes occurred around JW. Mainly the fainting spells but also her tendencies to go all shy around him- especially in group tasks and German where she had to do her best to impress him, like not being late to class because of Chatterbox.

"Who is Chatterbox?" Richard Galloway enquired skeptically, his bushy untamed eyebrows raised. "Melissa claims is the reason for her two latenesses to her classes but I cannot fathom why. Is it a

Robot or some sort of strange euphemism for ladies things?" he added, Melissa blushed as her Guidance teacher burst out laughing.

"Oh no-no! No-no!" Mrs Elliott chortled, a tear of laughter in her eye. She composed herself, and replied with her hands clasped together in an angelic pose. "It's an unfortunate nickname the pupils have given to the redheaded Punk girl in their class. She's the reason a couple of the teachers are running late actually, well, her mother is," the Guidance teacher added in a hushed tone. She motioned in the direction of the redheaded all-female family congregating on the other side of the Assembly hall. Their eyes fall upon the mother and daughter who were rather animatedly chewing the ear off of the poor young Mrs Riddoch. Melissa felt disappointed not to see her favourite buddy. She thought about the appointment coming next with her Drama teachers. She was dreading the personal questions most of all and was so taken over by it, she didn't hear her father and teacher lavishing praise on her. They thought she was just being modest and said their goodbyes with all smiles.

"What a wonderful woman! You're a good little girl, Melly, don't you forget," Richard remarked as they strode towards the waiting area sat in front of the two drama teachers. Their two tables were directly in front of the stage and the hall clock so Melissa could count the seconds away.

"Dad, you're embarrassing me," was all Melissa could say as her father hugged her. He rarely hugged her at home so hugging her in school was just bizarre. Richard sighed his apology and removed his arm. He fixated on the piece of paper with the map and timetable for teacher's evening; the Parent evening guide.

The hall itself had teachers arranged in seats and desks borrowed from classrooms. One seat for the pupil and two extra ones for the parents if they were both in attendance. However, it was assumed each pupil was only attending with one parent to allow for other commitments. Each desk was clearly labelled with the department and if that was not enough there were extra maps for the parents in each Parents evening guide. The waiting area was a large square of chairs in the centre of the school assembly hall. Each chair linked together with interlocking metal hooks- these were a death-trap for children's fingers but they quickly learnt not to try to pry the chairs apart. It had no sharp edges, but it left bruises on unwitting pinkies.

Melissa tapped on the sides of her chair and focused all of her attention on the clock.

"Tempus Motus in Latin. I simply ask the Goddess to lend me the power to move from one place to another. It's a matter of concentrating and controlling your breathing."

Melissa thought back to when her aunt had explained briefly her powers over the summer. Her Dad sighed again and halted her tapping.

"It's time, come on," he nudged her off the seats. They approached Mrs Bright with hesitation. Richard steeled his nerves, he was prepared for this conversation.

"The opposite of Richard's power, which is premonition, his consciousness gets taken out of his body where he cannot control his breathing and can only concentrate on the past or future image he is being shown."

Melissa could hear her auntie speaking much more clearly if she closed her eyes but it was difficult to concentrate with all the noises around them in the assembly hall. She wished she could be at home watching her favourite shows on TV.

"Melissa had us all really worried last month. That was an alarming thing to happen, in all my years as a drama teacher I've never had to deal with a first year student passing out on us. Neither has Miss Cox, isn't that right, Audrey?" the teacher enquired, her voice loud and clear as she projected to her neighbour.

"Oh yes, of course, thought we'd had to call an ambulance," Miss Cox agreed. Melissa certainly wished she could stop time; Richard put on a brave face and gave his best impression of a doctor as he explained to them what had happened. His words left Melissa feeling mortified.

"It's alright, she's been to the doctors since then and it's certainly a family trait, so to speak. Melissa and I both suffer from occasional narcolepsy. Her fainting happens without any known reason, no matter how much she has eaten or slept. It is less likely to happen if she is relaxed, so a stress-free teaching environment is recommended."

Miss Cox looked almost appalled at this bald-faced disclosure. Mrs Bright's eyes wrinkled in concern.

"Oh dear, that's not good at all, I'll try my hardest to help Melissa in whatever way I can," Mrs Bright gestured beseechingly with her hands. It looked as if she was about to get onto the stage and start singing like Whoopi Goldberg in *Sister Act*. Melissa could picture her Drama teacher up on a stage. She probably had started out as a professional actor before becoming a teacher, Melissa realised.

"It's all written in the letter I sent to the nurse along with the doctors reports. But we're not here to talk about all this. Anyway, thank you for your concerns," Richard said genuinely, glancing over at Miss Cox. Thankfully, she was talking to another parent. He smiled inwardly, teachers never changed.

"Aye, yes, Melissa, she's been doing well. I encourage everyone to be considerate of her and she performs well in the group activities. The class recently started on a project that we do with all first years; it's where we re-enact a Victorian classroom during the First World War and have the pupils take on a persona of that time."

"That sounds exciting, Melissa enjoyed learning about Anne Frank and watching the videos in History class," Richard offered, holding his arms close to his chest, listening carefully. He liked to watch documentaries on wars; Melissa thought. In fact, Richard was trying to figure out if there was any reason to worry about the fainting spell, as it had not been questioned it seemed the teachers were buying into the idea, as had the doctors.

"As it coincides with some of what they have been learning in other classes Melissa's even presented some ideas during the group discussion although I sense reluctance in speaking up. I think she's gifted, if only she could overcome the shyness."

Richard agreed. Melissa tuned out of the conversation for the remaining three minutes, until her father stood up and shook this teacher's hand, she had been comfortably content with staring at the clock. It was her new friend, this clock. Although, she couldn't help it when she smiled upon standing up. JW was there.

"Well, you seem as relieved as I am to be done with them. German next yes?" He asked quietly, walking Melissa reluctantly from the hall. "I need to pop to the loos first, wait here, we've got a few minutes before the next appointment."

"Okay, Da," Melissa mumbled, glad to have the time to mull about and relieved to have a moment to herself away from her teachers. It was the beginning of December, they would be free from school in a couple weeks, and Melissa had her Birthday before the winter break. Two weeks away from school could not come soon enough. While she was preoccupied with this thought her eyes drifted slowly towards a familiar Dutch boy as her ears prickled.

"...kijk naar al deze leraren..." she could hear float through from the assembly hall. She stared, despite herself, wondering what the words meant. It certainly was not German like the class they had together with Perry. She tuned into the conversation.

"Mam, kunt u spreken Engels?"

"Sorry, mein Zoon, I know people here think being bilingual is absurd. I understand how you don't want to stand out, but honestly it's not like anyone really cares," The woman he had called Mam replied in a sophisticated, perfect accent, like her son's.

"Mamma," JW sighed with exasperation. The Mother and son sat in the seats, presumably waiting for Mr Murtagh, the head of Mathematics. Melissa slightly envied his aptitude for numbers, when she was not busy eavesdropping on him; which was never something she ever did on purpose, of course.

80

JW and his Mother shared similar body shape and much about their aesthetics made them look alike. She was wearing an ankle length skirt, with a slit down each side, with a pair of brown boots and a V-neck cardigan. She carried on her lap a winter coat and a leather handbag. However, where his mother wore earthy colours like brown and green JW chose greys and black. The most similar thing about them both was their matching hairstyle. It was as if they had walked into the same hair dresser and asked for the same haircuts, Melissa realised. She could say it was funny how much alike they were, since they both had a Dutch accent and mid-blonde hair. Most classmates might have laughed at JW for his feminine characteristics, maybe even said what all teenage boys say, but Melissa shot those ideas out the window with the first mental boomerang. It was sweet, adorable, charming actually, how much alike he was to his Mammy, she thought. She pretended not to stare so intently and instead willed a cloak of invisibility and for time to stand still.

"Melissa, let's go!" Richard Galloway piped up.

"Dad!" Melissa yelped, clearly startled. JW flinched slightly, looking straight at her face. His eyes. The boomerang slapped Melissa with the idea, he might be able to pass as his Mother if her put on makeup and high heels. She stifled a giggle as she followed her Father to the next teacher.

JW rushed quickly to hide his face. What was *she* doing *here*? He wondered, but then chastised himself for thinking something so stupid. Of course she was here- it was parent's night. He wondered if it was glaringly obvious right then he was embarrassed, he felt anxious some of the popular girls would hear his Mum speaking Dutch. They made fun of his accent in class enough, actually being seen talking the language could be a social death sentence.

"You must be Mrs Wouters?" Mr Murtagh said as he stood to offer his great big hand to JW's mother. Her fingers were small and delicate inside the teachers. "Pleasure to meet you," he added, with a charming smile. He looked the tall, blonde woman up and down, admiring her tanned slender figure. JW found another reason to blush as they sat down at the desk in front of the head of the Mathematics department.

"It's my pleasure, please call me Carla-Rose," she replied, laying her handbag and coat on the back of her chair before sitting down next to her son. JW knew his Mam well, she would appreciate anyone calling her name properly. It had taken all of her polite effort not to snarl at the German teacher, and instead had sat grinding her teeth in annoyance. A languages teacher not being able to pronounce a simple "ou" or "W" was an insult, and the way the two woman had approached each other JW could sense a great disturbance in the force. They would be at each other's throats at any future meeting that might occur.

"I must say, your accent is incredibly melodic, and your English is excellent, but then you probably hear that all the time," Mr Murtagh commented, he leant back in his chair and cupped his big hands together.

"Thank you, yes, it is as you say, I hear all the time," Carla-Rose mimicked, giving him a half-smile. JW sighed quietly and agreed. She had been told her English was exceptional for years now, and was just over the space of one Parent's night. It was starting to get on his

82

nerves. Mr Murtagh ignored the boy's reaction and cleared his throat, giving Mrs Wouters his full attention.

"I must say JW is an exceedingly bright boy, he's greatly advanced for a first year, and I'm already sensing that his future will be an easy path academically. Are you good at mathematics yourself?"

"Oh yeah, he has, you could say, learnt from the best," Carla-Rose remarked fluidly, she crossed her legs in a way the slit of her skirt fell open where it revealed a great deal of her smooth legs. JW turned his head away bashfully, his mother was so infuriating tonight. He wished she had just stormed out after the meeting with his German teacher, that way he would have been at home instead of watching her flirting with his Mathematics teacher. Thankfully they only spoke for the allotted five minutes and he was able to inject more enthusiasm into their meeting with the Music teacher.

"Hi Mr C! This is my Mum, Carla-Rose!" he beamed, after they had bounced over to the location of the solitary Music department where his teacher sat all by himself.

"Hello," His Mother replied instinctively, shaking his hand and then sat down.

"Good evening; JW is a particularly outgoing student, I've been quite happy to have him in my class the last few months. He says he's had a Guitar instructor at home?"

"Oh yeah, his step-dad has been encouraging him to learn guitar so we have an instructor from the Steiner school come over twice a week. He got his first acoustic guitar for his birthday and has actually been begging for an electric for Christmas for months."

"Oh really, wow, keep it up. There's not many parents in this town who actively take interest. Music is a fantastic outlet for teenagers and in years to come he could be superbly confident from it. I know, many pupils use Music as a way to slack off in school, but please keep up the good work with your instructor, Josef."

The rest of the evening followed a similar pattern with JW being told he was a genius and Carla-Rose saying "Oh yeah, he is" in one way or another. They bumped into Perry with his parents and took a great excuse to sulk off for a breather. At around the time he spotted Melissa with her Dad talking to Jordan's Mum in the Social Area. He had seen their parents a couple times together but hadn't realised before that they were more than just neighbours. He caught them talking later on when he was walking with his Mum out to the car; a bright blue Picasso mini-van belonged to his step-Dad, Fritz. It had been parked at the front of the school across the road. Melissa appeared to be arguing with her father.

"...But Dad, it's not like that!" He could hear her whining, and it shocked him for two reasons. The first was he had never heard her speak that loudly; the second being he was actually eavesdropping on her, as if he actually cared. Although, he was curious and carried on listening in.

"Well, Mel, I feel like you need the chance to progress and find your own path. Have you been writing like I suggested?" it was harder to hear Richard Galloway from the car because he was not as emotional as his teenage daughter.

"Yes, Da, I have," she grumbled, her high-pitched voice mirrored the one her best friend often used when she was upset. JW though, he couldn't hear the next thing Melissa said, could have sworn it was about the fainting incident.

"Times like this might happen again, and that's why you write, it'll help. In time you will deal with it like I did, like we all do, and it becomes a normal part of growing up."

"Yeah, well, I wish I could stop time!" Melissa yelled unexpectedly, stomping away, pushing her Dad back so he stumbled before he could run after her.

"Only *The Tempest* could do..." JW could hear Richard say, detecting fear in his voice, before they two had disappeared from his range of hearing.

Chapter Seven
Friendships

Louise was alone in Melissa's bedroom one Saturday afternoon while her friend went to use the shower in the family bathroom. This was when she spotted a purple ruler-lined notebook her friend used regularly as a drawing pad. It was wire-bound and held together with a clip. Having no regard for Melissa's privacy, because they were best friends after all, Louise opened the book and flipped through it. She saw the sketches, doodles and caricatures Melissa had drawn to show her regularly and flicked through them to look for anything new. She was curious about a page that appeared to be hand written and seemed to be a diary. She saw the mention of JW but expected the rest of the entry to be pandering and overwhelmingly mushy nonsense. But then she noticed mention of Dublin and- then, rapidly, before she could stop herself, she read the whole thing-

~~October 29th~~ December 6th

My Dad said I should start a Book of Shadows so I decided to turn this old Drawing pad into one. I have seen his and couldn't understand them, he says I SHOULD know Theban by now, but I don't. I've only been learning a bit of basic stuff anyway since ~~they~~ "Dropped the bomb"

I guess I should start off by saying... My mammy died the same year

I turned seven, during the summer, and at the funeral my Gram kept

saying: "You're supposed to die before your children." And yeah true, but

before then life was A-Okay, we had the funeral, a bunch of family visited

from Dublin, and when Dad and ~~me~~ got back life started to get weird. I

met ~~Craig~~, one of my friend's stepbrothers, he bullied me for a while, and I

kept running from him of course.

Louise paused in her reading to check if her friend was still in the shower. Melissa often took a long time so her best friend could determine how long she had to read for. At this point Louise was aware the sort of things she was reading were all things she had not listened to Melissa about. She felt like a truly bad friend for not listening but also carried on reading because she had already gotten this far with it.

My Granma said she wanted me raised Catholic because I had been

Christened in a Roman Catholic church, but my Mum's will stated she

wanted me raised the way my Dad's family wanted, as a Wiccan. Bullying,

running away, they were making fun of me because my Mum died from

Cancer. *My friends turned on me and my oldest friend still doesn't*

understand my reactions back then, I guess I can't do much at that age

can I? I was just a scared kid, but of course I'll tell myself there is always

something worse.

But it still astounded having Magick in my life I start now, and after months at the Academy I am thinking 'How can I be a Wiccan and a student here. With all these horrid people!' this is how my day went by the way for the most parts since just now It's Break time and I am at school.

I was on my way to school when I crossed Lewis road and walked down ST. Catherine's road, to Fleurs place when I felt a presence of something or someone. I turned round, saw Perry and JW [JW has weird hair because he bleached it and the colour is a bit Oak-coloured but in the heavy light of the PE hall it looks grey] were walking toward me - more straight in my direction - suddenly the world went into slow motion and then my sight was blocked when I had a premonition; Perry was asking me out not for him but for JW; my eyes went back into focus and Perry was frantically waving his hand at me. I hit him on the back of the head with my BOS. James whom was standing across the street was laughing then two blonde 'models' walked past and he followed them. My straight black hair [which I had dyed this colour a while ago] hangs at shoulder length. JW's gorgeous greyish-green eyes met my ~~small-pupil-ed,~~ deep brown eyes and I quickly turned and carried on with my morning walk, to school.

If you wonder why I don't have any friend's -Because I am just so stupid. -MG

Louise felt particularly hurt by the last thing. Her best friend. Not calling *her* best friend? They had been through all childhood things together. It was utterly hurtful. Especially since they saw each other every other day. Instead of getting overly emotional about it Louise just turned to the front cover and grabbed a gel pen.

"AHH! What are you doing?" Melissa enquired when she came into her bedroom, a large red bath towel around her torso and her brown hair bedraggled and wet.

"Just giving you a book protection, see? Now people will not try to open if you draw a knife on the cover!" Louise said, giddily.

"Or, they will think I'm mental and avoid me?" Melissa replied, skeptically, wriggling her eyebrows in confusion as she examined the drawings. "Keep out or I will kill you. SERIOUSLY!" Melissa laughed evilly, clutching the towel around herself.

"Classic right?!" Louise guffawed, adding in a maniacal laugh of her own. They took turns saying the phrase in different voices. Louise tried it in deep manly voices and mimicked pop-culture actors and accents- like Robocop.

"Keep Oot, Or I Vill Kill Vou!" Melissa hissed, "SEVIOUSVY!" She added, when she had slipped on some underwear she used the towel as a cape. "I Vill Suck Vor Bloooood!" She added in case it wasn't obvious she was pretending to be a vampire.

"You're so childish!" Louise exclaimed cackling, backing away from Melissa who tried to suck at her neck. They crawled on the bed. She allowed her friend to get on top of her and blow raspberries into the side of her neck.

"Na, you're the one who's the most childish," Melissa replied.

"Oh, and yourself? Maybe I'll challenge you to a pillow fight eh?" Louise remarked, grabbing the blue bed cushion from behind her back. Bringing it over so swiftly that Melissa dropped the towel so she could defend her face from the sudden whoosh of the pillow. She grabbed the second matching pillow and stood up off the bed; onto the blow up airbed Louise always used when she slept over in her room. It wheezed under her weight but the fabric was warm against her bare toes.

"If that's how the cookie crumbles," she replied.

"Oh, we should have cookies after, but first-!" -the pillow hit her square in the face with a soft whoosh of her hair.

"Goooood Morning! This is Barry bringing you the weather with MFR! The weather today is not a positive outlook. A wet morning is promised with icy roads ahead so be careful while driving this morning on your way to work or bringing the kids to school!" Sang the chirpy radio forecaster over the radio in their registration classroom. Melissa sat with her classmates; Chloe, Alisha, Johanna and AJ- who was sitting in the corner spritzing herself with Charlie body spray.

"Pwah! That bongs, Chatterbox do you really have to spray everywhere?" Asked one of the boys, the blond haired Corey Black, as he held his nose. The scent of cherries filled the air and Melissa preferred it to the smell of nicotine her classmate had before they came into the registration classroom. The other girls displayed no reaction to the smell and ignored Corey while the five boys in their class joined in with pretending they were hypersensitive to the smell. Melissa thought they all looked rather pathetic holding their noses and pulling sour faces.

"Really? I keep saying I like to be called AJ because it stands for Ally Jackson. All the guys like you insist I'm supposed to be called that?" AJ replied; or Chatterbox, which ever becomes easier to remember, Melissa thought to herself. The group of boys laughed and the three girls- Chloe, Alisha and Johanna- glanced at each other, not sure if they were allowed to say anything.

"It's because in all classes, when you turn up for them that is, you talk incessantly," Ms Harrison the English teacher who took their registration class declared as she sat up at her desk and leant back in her chair. Ms Harrison was middle-aged, with greying frizzy brown hair and small round glasses. She had a tendency to dress in black. Her usual routine every morning was to take the register, join in with the banter, and turn on the radio. The one exciting task during the mornings of December had been since when she had given Corey the first chocolate on the class advent calendar- which went by alphabetical order until, naturally, the first person who had a birthday in December. The boys stopped laughing and decided to talk to each other separate from the girls. AJ harrumphed and immediately became the head of the conversation with the corner of the room that the girls dominated- and she certainly talked incessantly like a chatterbox, never allowing others to say much more than a mumble or a grunt.

"I think my body spray is nice, don't you girls?"

"I think it smells nice," Alisha replied, and the others agreed.

"Well I bought it for myself this time. Last time my sister bought me it but I ran out of the bottle she gave me. I asked her for more but she said no. I tried to steal one but she moaned at me. So of course I had to go out and buy it with my own pocket money. I didn't steal it, I swear, I legit went out and bought some. I got the cherries and raspberries, these two-" she said, and pulled the two red and pink canisters from her school bag. They were mainly white except for the delicate girlish colours and patterns displayed on their labels. "Because they smelled nice, and so I bought them. I figure it's only polite to smell nice when I notice how I smell after having a cig..." she went on. Rambling. For the most part she seemed to be having a monologue...

Melissa sat up and stretched her arms. She looked around her History class, most of her classmates were in various stages of boredom from the film they had been made to watch and the teacher was nowhere to be seen. He was most likely in the staff room enjoying a tea or coffee with some chocolate digestives while he caught up on the latest gossip from his colleagues. The thoughts she had on her teachers whereabouts almost evaporated when the young Melissa's heavy eyes fell upon the object of her affection...

"Geeuw!" the Dutch boy yawned, covering his mouth politely.

There was JW sat over by the windows; one tanned, arm propped his head up, his sleeves rolled up to the elbow, and his droopy sea-green eyes were fixed on the screen in an attempt to look interested in what the class was supposed to be watching. His redheaded friend James was fast asleep, and snoring loudly, in the seat next to him, using his pencil case as a pillow, while Perry was the only one fully alert. Perry Leach tapped his feet in an effort to keep himself occupied. He sat prone, like a seagull in the playground when pupils were eating chips, eager for this period to end, one arm on the desk and the other draped across the back of his chair; his prawn-like, swimmers legs were on display because he was wearing his PE shorts (again, he was so odd).

Melissa looked back at herself to check she had not drooled in her sleep. Without even thinking she ran a hand through her coal, black hair. She found something gross and mushy entangled in the strands. Andrew, who sat behind her, burst out laughing in that exact moment. James woke up startled and everyone else stared over towards her. Andrew, the little devil, had put some chewing gum in Melissa's hair.

"What's so funny?" Perry asked, trying not to sound interested in the reply, as Andrew was a delinquent and they often were found arguing together outside class. Andrew laughed devilishly while beside himself his friend John told him to calm down because he didn't want them to get in trouble. Melissa blushed profusely.

At the end of class instead of getting food at break time she met up with Jade in the girl's bathroom who helped her to cut the chewing gum out of her hair. Jade was ever so calming and reassuring compared to the other students. She combed out Melissa's hair and they were alone for a couple of minutes sitting on a makeup desk next to the hand driers. Melissa could see herself in the mirror and sat beside Jade she looked like a child.

"So Mel, any idea what you might do after you leave school?"

"Um, well, I thought about it sometimes but really it's not crucial right now, is that okay?"

"Of course, I mean I didn't expect you to know. My sister used to want to be a Vet, but now she wants to be a waitress. Do you want to know what I'm planning to be?" Jade asked her, tugging gently on a knot in her hair. The first year appreciated the care she was taking and it was tremendously relaxing to have her hair brushed by someone else. Melissa nodded. "I'm going to be a tattoo artist, go to college next summer and do Fine Art," Jade replied, she put the brush down as Melissa turned to her in surprise.

"Really? People can do that?"

"Totally, if you work until your portfolio is good enough then have a tattoo artist look at it they can help you to get an apprenticeship in a professional tattoo studio. I've always wanted to do that, but ever since my Mum took me for my first tattoo for my Birthday, I've researched it a lot," Jade explained in more detail. She pulled up the sleeve of her sixth year jumper to allow Melissa to see a Ying-yang tattoo on her wrist. The small girl asked the usual questions like "did it hurt?" and Jade shrugged it off with a typical answer; "at first but after a few minutes it's just an irritation."

"Okay, cool, I always thought being into tattoos was really dodgy! Didn't know you could be... Qualified," Melissa emphasised. Wondering what she could get as she gawked at the ink. If she did want a tattoo it would have to be small, well hidden, mainly because she was raised to be against any modifications to the body due to Bible teachings, as it went against God's human design.

"Yeah, that's cos lots of Forresian tattoo guys are scratchers, like they don't get into it the proper way, do it for drugs or give really bad tatts. It's a shame, you can be really good sometimes but if you do tattoos without the proper qualification you could get in real trouble," Jade went on, a sour look on her face showed she knew a lot of people like that.

"Wait, you're not eighteen yet? How do you have a tatt?" Melissa asked hurriedly. Anxious to change the mood and cheer up her buddy. Jade turned and hopped off the counter onto the floor, she turned around and smirked.

"Boy, you catch on fast," Jade giggled. "Some guy's allow you to get a tatt if you're under age so long as you have a parent with you, but. Big. But. If they get caught there's a chance they could lose their license. So for that reason, overall it's helpful to have a good relationship with your tattoo place. It's all about trusting them to do their job and provide a quality piece of art."

"Cool, you've made me think tattoos are cool," Melissa beamed, she slid from the counter top holding onto the older girls hands to steady her. "I totally want one!"

"Excellent, I would hope so. Hey, how about when I eventually become a badass professionally qualified tattooist I give you your first tattoo for free? How would you like that?"

"Sure, I would love you to!" Melissa squeaked.

"Only if you want to, when the time comes of course," Jade added, holding the eleven year old at arms-length. Melissa nodded smiling with excitement.

During December it was birthdays all round, their Christmas movie was The Grinch and so they watched in the mornings instead of listening to the Radio, and as before everyone was allowed Advent chocolate. Corey Black had his Birthday first, right after parent's night, he was given the Advent day chocolate by Mrs H in Registration class. The following Sunday was Melissa's birthday and she had the Advent chocolates for both days to make up for the time they had off for the weekend. She was pleased to not have to be sang "Zum Geburtstag viel Glück!" In German class, it was embarrassing enough to have it sang at you in English. Unfortunately for Alisha she had to suffer through the Birthday song in French.

"It was so embarrassing, she just had to do it," Alisha grumbled. She was happy to receive presents from her classmates and friends, as well the special extra treats were especially wonderful, but the Birthday song in every single lesson was overly traumatising. Their buddies were all missing and one Sixth year had explained to them they had taken a hard crash after the Christmas Dance. Although, he was dressed at Santa Claus and handing out cards and sweets, so the childish first years were taking what he said with a pinch of sugar and accepted his candy canes instead. Although, it did explain why they were able to have an ordinary conversation without Chatterbox, the class gossip machine.

"Tell them about what happened in Music last week?" Jordan nudged snappishly, turned towards the girls table. Every other boy in the class seemed to be in a state of innocent confusion, busying themselves with eating junk food which was donated freely by the school faculty. They sat huddled around the Television in Registration on the last day of school watching the final fifteen minutes of The Grinch on the Video player. Meanwhile, Melissa and most of her female classmates were using the last day of school as an excuse to dress up in holiday themed jewellery and makeup they had helped each other with applying. She was wearing a pair of sparkly star earrings with purple eye liner.

"What do you mean?" Johanna asked, curiously.

"James was being really excited and you know *James,*" Jordan explained to his classmates.

"And we have Music today too," Melissa mumbled, her friends in her class gasped and looked to Alisha for her response.

"He sat next to me in music as well, on my birthday," Alisha hinted, taking a suspense filled pause. "This one time we were listening to some operatic type music and he got off his chair and down on one knee again where he proceeded to mime-sing me the music romantically to me," she answered the expectant eyes, blushing under her blue eyeshadow.

"These were jokes, he wasn't 'wooing' me or anything, and he was just trying to be funny. Don't look at me like that," Alisha reprimanded, Johanna and their gang rolled their eyes.

"Sounds like Romeo and Juliet to me," injected their Registration teacher, who seemed to have been the only person watching the film while the rest of the class participated in the conversation.

"It didn't hurt me though cos I also found it funny and liked the funny attention," Alisha remarked. "So it's not like Romeo and Juliet."

"Oh it so is," Jordan blurted out.

"What do you know?" Johanna asked. The small boy blushed.

"I know nothing," he stated rapidly, turning quickly away from the girls to stare at the credits as the bell rang to signal the end of Registration.

"You know something," Johanna bubbled, chasing him from the room as he tried to run away with his rucksack slung over his arm.

Unfortunately the amount of winter garments he was wearing slowed him down and she managed to catch up to him before his first class.

Tempus Motus... Moving through time was the second thing Melissa obsessed over, aside from thinking about school work or her crush.

"Are you stalking JW?" James had asked her in the Social Area one Lunch period. Of course she had denied it. Although, she wanted nothing more than to stop time and get close to her crush. However much she wanted that to happen it was outside of her abilities.

Music came surprisingly quickly, it arrived in such a drag it was as if she had fallen into a coma right after Registration and woke at the end of lunch bell, Melissa thought. She drifted into the queue outside the classroom with minimal discomfort. It was then the guys all rushed through the fire exit door.

"Melissa? Do you never eat lunch?" Jordan asked, clocking eyes with his neighbour. She shrugged and they leant against the brick wall together. JW and his friends looked at her warily. James stood on her other side, separating her from her view of JW.

"Well, two weeks away from the weirdos in this class will be great," Perry guffawed at his own comment.

"You mean like you?" James snapped, glancing at Melissa. She knew who Perry meant and it was definitely her. Ever since her fainting spells had started people had been speaking about her with more and more paranoia. Over the last few months she had become the topic of wide-spread gossip. It might as well have been front page news in the Forres Gazette. It had yet to find a line in the Press and

Journal. Despite that, everyone knew about her fragility and they were pretty mean about it.

"Perry, leave it, would you?" Jordan added, pushing himself off the wall. There was now a wall made of the red headed James and his shorter tanned friends.

"Oh and it's your clingy cheese brothers. Look, Josef," Perry motioned, turning round to face his friend and their Music teacher, Mr C.

"Mr Leach, please wait patiently outside the auditorium, you're making a scene. Also, the fire exit is not an entrance. You abusing it, as such, triggers a silent alarm. Please just shut up, I have no patience for the likes of you today," their teacher explained. Melissa smiled to herself as she watched Perry gawping like a fish. The boy with the glasses saw her expression and his eyes narrowed into a glare. They leant against the wall as before. After their teacher unlocked the doors he motioned for them to enter the auditorium.

"You won't be sitting at the keyboards today. I'd like you all to sit at the tables. Please feel free to play on the Xylophones, like the children you are," Mr C grumbled. "I'm going to tutor Mark on the piano today, he's volunteered to practice in front of you this afternoon. I know you'll all enjoy, he's quite talented," the teacher rambled, aware once they had entered the classroom would soon mostly ignore him. First years, he grumbled.

"Xylophones, rock on!" James cheered, stumbling into a seat beside JW. Jordan sat opposite him beside Melissa and JW found himself sitting opposite her. She blushed, naturally. He smiled awkwardly.

"Where do I sit?" Perry asked quietly, his face going chalk white.

"Why, wherever you wish Mr Leach," the teacher replied bluntly. He surely did not give a damn.

Perry sighed. He was then hemmed in on the opposite side of the tables from his best friend; surrounded by the girls in their class he got on well with and a couple of the boys whom he detested. Once the entire class was in attendance Mark took his place at the grand piano next to the teacher. He required little instruction to play a perfect selection of Christmas melodies.

"He's pretty darn good, look at him over there, surrounded by girls, geez. Melissa? How come you're not enthralled by him too?" JW asked her, a hint of jealousy in his voice. Melissa had been watching but as the piano was behind her it was difficult to do so without twisting her body.

"He's good, but I'd much rather not get a crick in my neck," she admitted, JW gave her a coy half-smile.

"Sure, right," He smirked. "Even Alisha is taken by him, dang older boys."

"Wheeshed," James hissed.

"She certainly likes gingers," Melissa added under her breath.

"Oh, you've got him there, look he's blushing now," Jordan pointed out to her, his arm draped over her chair on top of her school bag and winter coat.

"Harsh bro," James grumbled sounding oddly hurt.

"Sorry bro," Jordan replied, pouting.

"You always do, daft cunt," James mumbled, just loud enough for people to hear. He looked furious but as Jordan leant across the table to apologise again they were interrupted.

"Language!" The teacher bleated out of nowhere.

"He has super hearing. I swear," JW muttered to Melissa, who giggled in reply. Jordan and James amused themselves by playing with the xylophones as a way of making up when they weren't bickering.

"Hey, any special plans for Friday night?" JW asked Melissa, leaning across the table and putting his head in his hands. His grey eyes were tired from a long week at school and Melissa noticed his pupils were oddly dilated.

"Friends tonight, I've been watching it all season. I can't wait to find out what happens next," she added with excitement.

"You watch Friends? That's my all-time favourite show!"

"Mine too!" James interrupted. Jordan shushed him, grabbing James hands and turning his attention back to their conversation.

"Okay, anyway, how shocked were you about Monica and Chandler?" JW continued, leaning towards Melissa once more.

"Super shock! Totally cute couple though," she responded, mirroring his posture. For a moment she forgot where they were and they bonded over their favourite television show.

"I bet you anything she'll marry him, and then Ross will end up with Rachel. Like I'm fed up with the divorces stuff, it's so irritating to watch," JW reasoned. He was meeting eye contact with Melissa for the first time; not as weird as he had expected. In fact she was wearing eyeshadow and glittery earrings, it was quite pretty.

"I predict it'll be something crazy, like Rachel will have his baby and they'll steal Monica's thunder. Ross needs to learn too, divorces is not a cool superpower," Melissa added. She was aware of the tiny bubble of anticipation growing in her chest, like all her dreams had come true and she wanted to cry from happiness.

"Hey you ever wonder what member of the Friends group you are?" he asked, aware that he hadn't stuttered for a while. Normally talking to girls made him stutter a lot. He felt relaxed talking to Melissa. Unusual, but a good feeling. Like she was a guy.

"I think if you're not Chandler or Joey then you're not a boy," She answered playfully. "Like Rachel, with the hair before and everything," she added cheekily, sticking out her tongue and crossing her eyes.

"Oh thanks," JW rolled his eyes sarcastically. "I was going to be nice and say you were like Monica, but then, hey Rachel is hot so I'll take that as a compliment... How you doin'?" he quoted the character and even winked. Melissa giggled. He was Joey if he did, she thought.

"Who wants to be Monica? Are you calling me a control freak? Have you seen my jotters? I'm zero percent neat-freak!" She mock gasped in response. JW seemed to consider this.

"Yeah, you're all over the place sometimes, but otherwise, anything is a lot neater than my scrawl," he finally said.

"Okay, you could be a doctor with your handwriting which is a good thing. So what's your diagnosis? Who am I?" Melissa asked, trying her best to keep the apprehension out of her voice.

"Phoebe, of course, my friend," JW expressed, folding his arms and leaning away from her.

"Woah! Oh see, I like the sound of that. Yes, I'm so totally Phoebe," She giggled to herself.

"Diagnosis, yeah, and I'm totally Joey! I'm Dr Drake Remoray!" JW inflicted a slight Italian accent as he spoke. "How you doin'?" he asked again, encouraging Melissa to giggle even more.

"I'm good, baby, how you doin'?" she squeaked back.

If only time could capture this moment...

Chapter Eight
Solstice

"What are you doing here?" I asked myself as I looked in the mirror. To tell the truth, I in truth dislike Scotland. It is truly cold in generally and the weather is awful, even more so in December. Wales, yes is just as bad on the coast but in Cardiff it's a well-protected city rarely gets much more than a light battering from the winds. Although, it is a lot more similar to home than England, and I hate England with an abundant passion.

"Excuse me?" the old woman asked, as she burst into the bathroom, flabbergasted I was stood in there, as I am in fact a man. Public restrooms, well they never changed.

"You didn't see me," I reasoned in return, my voice swift as a snake to its prey.

"I didn't see you," she replied obediently, her eyes glazed over. With that she ran into the nearest cubicle and slammed the door in a hurry. She yanked down her bottoms and proceeded to pee intolerably loudly. That was my turn to run out of there.

"Quentin!" Melinda gasped when she bumped into me then. I had been waiting around for her in the Forres Community Centre because I had managed to convince her parents I could collect her from her gymnastics class and I was a hundred times more reliable than her *pathetic* public transport. She gazed at me for another second before she lobbed her school bag at my face.

I began to protest, it was not my intention to be her book mule. I noticed her sweaty leggings and other tight fitting gym clothes she was wearing. Pink striped down the sides, black panel down the middle and purple sweat bands on either wrist. Her brown frizzy hair bunched up into a lazy pony tail. Matching trainers completed the look.

"You are a lifesaver! I am so beat, I couldn't manage to call a taxi in this condition, and the buses to Alves are cancelled. My friends *had* to bail on me to go to youth club. It's ridiculous," she moaned. For a heavy second I remembered she was still a teenage girl Melinda. She would be a fully-fledged adult in a few short months, in the New Year.

"No worries, honey, I'll have you home in a jiffy. You can shower and I'll make you some hot choc, it'll be lush. You'll see," I told her, gushing out platitudes.

"I love it when you say lush, it makes you sound so Welsh. You're like my Welsh Gay best friend," Melinda teased. I tried to hide a snarl the same way I had to when I used to watch her with Dean. She would dote on Dean and her little boy friends like they were her extended family, her brothers. She treated me like an older brother because I was a temporary lodger in her parent's house. The Barnes' are nice people, too bad for them I came to join their coven this year...

Yule is an important time of year. The coven celebrates it in the same way as the other big Wiccan and Pagan holidays but it was the only one where mulled wine and traditional Christmas foods and drinks were acceptable. The winter solstice is the shortest day of the year, when the sun rises late and sets earlier. Logically, because of the extended darkness it is also cold, below freezing. This winter solstice was not to be so cold. This was the time of year when I could stop being invisible. Melinda was mine.

"What the fuck is *he* doing here?"

The voice belonged to Dean. It catapulted me out of my daydreaming into reality. The double doors into the reception area of the community centre were behind us as we stood outside in the freezing cold December weather. I could feel my car eagerly awaiting us in the car park at the back of the building.

"Well? What is he doing here?" Dean asked again. His voice rising. Melinda gasped at him, completely speechless. As usual, in this situation, she became a useless fumbling idiot.

"It's the little twerp," I replied, taking a firm step in front of her to stand over him. He was missing a growth spurt and I was a fully grown seventeen year old. I felt his hand coming out then, clenched into a fist. I grabbed it with ease. "Really?" I sighed with exasperation at the poor little teen's plight.

"You shouldn't be with him, Melinda," Dean reasoned, his voice high pitched. He looked past me towards her, his teeth grinding in anger. It was rude he would not look at me so I tightened my grip on his hand. He winced and pulled away. Weak Dean.

"Go find your friends," Melinda demanded.

Chapter Nine

Louise started to write down her thoughts in a journal, she considered what Melissa had written but decided against it. Thinking too much, she reasoned, this is not some sort of autobiography, it was just a simple diary.

"I feel really melodramatic," she admitted, to her border collie. They were sitting on her bed listening to the country music channel. "It's my best friend's birthday and here I am worrying about her instead of asking a dumb question. It shouldn't be so hard, right?" she baffled the dog. The black and white pup simply nuzzled up to her; dog hair didn't bother her at all, although it was a pain to remove the white fur from her black clothes.

She wrote the main thing on her mind...

15/12/02

Melissa C. Galloway likes a boy who everybody calls JW. She can't ask him out, because he is friends with our arch enemy, Jordan.

Oh yeah, and she's a witch, (but she didn't know until she was ten,) four years after her mum died from chest cancer. The only people who knew her Mum had died came from her primary school and a few boys from her primary school liked to bully her because of it; they even managed to get two girls from their F class who just did it to be popular and didn't really know Melissa's mammy had died.

"Sounds cool, right babe?" she asked showing the journal entry to her dog. The pet sniffed it and gave a spritely tail wag in response. "Yeah, I'll just finish it off, then we'll head out," Louise reasoned. The dog leapt from the bed, surprisingly full of energy that hadn't been visible before, because she knew her mistress would soon be taking her for a walk.

While at the other primary school in the area Jw got bullied because he couldn't stand up for himself very well, (he has got two friends James and Perry). Melissa has her best friend Louise, ~~who is also a witch,~~ and her new Secondary school friends Angela, Chloe and various other chicks. ~~So far Louise and their families were the~~

only people who knew Melissa was a witch.

Recently Melissa had started to keep a Journal for witches called the Book of Shadows. Witches kept them to write about spells and stuff.

Although, Melissa doesn't know about this stuff yet...

It had been a month since Louise had started to keep her journal and she found it oddly therapeutic. Although, unlike with Melissa it certainly was not a Book of Shadows. The last thing she had written about was their trip to the shops for New Year's Deals and then she put it away when school started. How often she would see Melissa with her purple spiral bound note book in school was uncountable.

"What are you daydreaming about?"

"Ugh, I do not daydream!" Louise defended. Her Dad was sat at the breakfast table reading his morning newspaper. He had a cup of strong coffee on the table in front of him and was looking at the Sports section. In their family they were passionate supporters of Rangers and yet when Forres Mechanics played also strove to follow the home team. The kitchen was decorated with Roosters and other farm themed brick-a-brack around the main kitchen counters and pantry. Beside the fridge in the corner was a two-foot tall gold fish tank mounted on a short bookshelf. The bookshelf housed Football books and cookbooks. Under the breakfast table was one of the dogs lying down across her feet, the black and white border collie Jess. The older dog, Tara the terrier, was snoozing contently in the dog bed in the hallway. On the wall behind her father, Alan Owens, she could read the clock and the Rangers calendar hung up to display January 2003.

"I better go see if Mel is ready for school," she groaned brusquely, nudging the dog off her feet before she pushed her chair back. Jess whined following her into the hallway. Her father slurped the coffee in approval.

"Give us a holler if you girls want a lift," Alan shouted through the house. Louise rushed through, her school bag slung over her shoulder and gave him a thumbs up. She still had to do her makeup but was easily left to last minute after she brushed her teeth. She had gotten a pair of straighteners for Christmas and was the first thing she used every day before eating breakfast. It was a lot to do so she had to get up an hour and a half before Melissa did in. Melissa was so lucky, Louise thought, she doesn't have any siblings who spent hours in the bathroom every day.

"Hey! Anyone awake?" Louise called through the Galloway house, opening the main front door. She took off her shoes and coat as she entered the house, leaving her school bag on a hook. As she made her way into the Galloway hallway through the second entry door her face was hit by a delicious warmth. After being outside for two minutes it was welcoming. She sauntered through the house into the living room where Richard was eating cereal in his armchair.

Unlike at her house, the Galloways never ate breakfast in the kitchen and only actually used the dinner table when guests were over for tea.

"Morning, Mel up?" she asked her best friend's Dad.

"Morning Lulu!" Richard said, almost startled by the newcomer. Louise grimaced at her nickname. She waved at him and sat down in front of the television. BBC Breakfast was on and there was a Celebrity on getting interviewed. Unless it was anyone from an American Romance film, Louise never paid attention. The only time she ever watched British actors was if they were young and attractive.

"Morning..." Melissa mumbled as she ambled downstairs a few minutes later. She was fully dressed already and was about to go into the bathroom when Louise grabbed her by the arm and dragged her into the kitchen. "No! What are you doing, stop," Melissa protested.

"You gotta' eat breakfast girl, come on," Louise insisted.

"No, I ate breakfast yesterday," Melissa mumbled.

"Oh none of that! You're eating today if you don't want to faint and be laughed at by the twerps at school," Louise continued as she shuffled through the pantry for cereal and brought Melissa a bowl of coco pops. She then opened the fridge to get the milk.

"You sound just like your Mum," Melissa whimpered, resting her head on the table. Her best friend brought her milk for the cereal and a glass of fresh orange juice.

"At least it's Mum and not Dad. If I behaved like you my Dad would pour ice water on my face in the mornings. Mum just yanks the covers off."

"Well, then can I please ask for Alan Jr. He's nice in the mornings," Melissa added to Louise's chagrin. Her lip pursed at the mention of her older brother, the favourite.

"He's a student now, the only time he gets up in the morning is to fall into the shower. His idea of a wake-up call is at two in the afternoon, and even then he'd just pour the Cheerio's and milk on my face, skipping the middle-man completely," Louise explained folding her arms under her chest. She handed a tablespoon to her friend and made her sit up to eat.

"He did only one time!" Melissa laughed. She fed herself the coco pops, just because Louise was watching. Her Dad came through to put his bowl away and find out what the joke was about.

"You put him up to it, didn't you?" Louise asked all of a sudden, leaning over the table.

"Ma-a-y-be," Melissa mumbled between mouthfuls.

"Oh yeah, I remember that story," Richard guffawed unpredictably.

"She was all like *My Hair* and screeching like a banshee," Melissa explained.

"My Hair!" she laughed the same as her father.

"I'm pleased to see you bond over, it took ages to get the smell of milk off my duvet," Louise grumbled. Richard patted her on the head as he left the room to sit down again. He had a slight limp these days and his knee was sore. It probably came from sitting down and looking at screens a lot, Louise wondered. Eventually he would need a walking stick if his sciatica got any worse. At least he didn't have narcolepsy like his daughter, Louise pondered.

"I'm sure your Mum washed it off," Melissa added, looking her best friend in the eye. Louise looked down at Melissa and could see she was wearing the new necklace she had gotten her for Christmas.

"Now finish your coco pops so we can go to school."

"Yes Mummy," Melissa replied with a cheeky grin.

On the way to school Melissa was wearing her new suede green body warmer under a faux fur trim cape. It was a fashionable upgrade from her old winter coat and made her look womanly. Louise and her mother had taken Melissa with them for the New Year sale and had gotten her fitted for her first bra. She needed it now. Both the girls were starting to fill out and look like adults up top. It matched with their hips. Over the winter break they had both paid the cost of blooming into womanhood all teenage girls have to suffer. It mostly involved lying down and watching movies, while consuming large amounts of chocolate.

"Melissa, why doesn't your auntie ever send clothes over from the States for me?" Louise asked, looking upon the outfit with envy.

"Because your parents can afford Debenhams maybe?" Melissa replied deadpanned. She rolled her eyes; Louise was constantly jealous of the treats and hand-me-downs Melissa would get from her Auntie Anne Galloway.

"Sorry I asked," Louise snapped back. They walked more until they met up with other school friends. They exchanged general pleasantries and wished each other a happy new year.

"Wow, nice clothes Mel," Chloe commented.

"What about my clothes?" Louise burst out with, her eyes were certainly turning green now. Chloe turned around on the taller girl and smiled. She appraised the cream coloured Parka and nodded.

"I love that, Debenhams right? My Mum has something similar," she replied. Melissa smiled in agreement.

"You look nice Lou, don't worry, your hairs straight too, look at her hair Chloe," she said for added measure. Louise looked to be calming down.

"Oh yeah, your hair is so shiny and straight. It looks so much longer now."

"Really Chloe?" Louise beamed. The other girls nodded.

They exchanged general chat until they made it to school. The whole way there Louise was thinking about the other necklace around her best friend's neck. Needless to say she had gotten her the diamond silver charm with a turquoise gemstone and matching earrings but the idea was spoiled by the other necklace. It was a pewter pentagram on an ugly leather rope. Why would she wear those together? Louise fumed. The two metals did not go together at all, she thought. It did not spring to her mind at that point a pentagram meant anything and she kept the thought to the back of her mind the whole way to school. They entered the building through the section with the boy's lockers and didn't even see who was behind them until they felt his eyes burning into the backs of their heads. Melissa stopped and they both turned around with hesitation.

"Wow," he said, his earlobes and tuffs of chestnut coloured hair sticking out from the bottom of his black beanie. The grey jeans and black shoes hidden under his knee length winter coat; which was army green, with insignia patches and had a fluffy hood. His grey eyes looked over the girls and as his eyes lingered on Louise she could see his pupils were dilated.

"Melissa?" She asked nudging her best friend. Louise looked at the poor boy with curiosity. She chanced a glance at Melissa and knew she was blushing.

"You look..." JW began to say his eyes stopping on Melissa's newly developed chest. His mouth raised into a coy half smile.

Chapter Ten

The push up bra came as a shock to JW. He had expected to see a few people dressed in new clothes because of the recent holiday. This was a big surprise on Melissa. In addition to the Hooch trousers, which were dark brown and tight around her... JW could hardly think of the words to describe it.

"Wow," he managed, flabbergasted. "You look..." He couldn't help it, the way she had gone from flat-chested to this over one fortnight defied words. Not absolutely massive because of course she was layered up in a strange array of mismatched and fluffy garments. Still, he wanted to see the improvements underneath. He mentally slapped himself for being such a pervert. Damn. Hormones.

"Da-yum, your girls look great," AJ proclaimed as she made her way over to them. JW noticed the smell on her breathe as the redheaded girl pushed him out of the way.

"You're here early, what's the rush?" Louise snarled, the two cherry-faced freckled girls stared each other down.

"Didn't your mummy ever teach you to take a sodding compliment?" AJ replied sharply. "I just wanted to tell Mel she looked cool in her new threads. Hey, a pentagram? You a witch?" she asked way too loudly, yanking at Melissa's necklace so it appeared from under her cape. JW blushed with jealousy, wondering if he would get away with something so daring, while staring at the necklace intently.

"Y-yeah, it is..." Melissa mumbled, struggling for words.

"She's not a witch!" Louise roared, making JW jump.

"Jesus, I was just asking, it's no biggie, chill the beans. My big sis has got one just like it, she tells me about these things, y'know? What's got you all twisted up? Can I not talk to Mel now, is that it?" she gabbled, after secreting the necklace again. JW felt anxious standing here now; on the one hand he wanted to talk to Melissa but on the other hand he felt awkward being close to Chatterbox.

"It's because you're a chatterbox, Chatterbox, and you SMOKE like a sodding chimney. Honestly have you never heard of a breath mint or deodorant for that matter? Go get some chuddy for Christ sakes!" Louise chortled, she knew how to talk to the master of rants, that was for sure, JW thought. He looked back at Melissa, she wore a frightened expression. It was a shame as when he saw her walking towards the school in her new clothes she had radiated confidence.

"Ugh, you better watch yourself girl, you don't know who you're messing with," was the last words he heard the redhead jeer before he snuck away.

At break time and lunchtime JW met up with his friends at the back of the school almost every day after getting food from either the vending machines in the social area or the canteen, as it was far too cold to go up the high street just yet. It was February now and the weather had finally gotten around to being cold enough to produce snow. This was an exciting time of year for the first years. First of all, their sixth year buddies were away for Prelims for the exams, so they were unmonitored and felt independent. Secondly, they had gotten into the groove of being in Secondary school and would soon be introduced to the next lot of first years. The best thing about going into second year, for JW, was soon he would be allowed to study more advanced sciences and other lesson subjects. Until then, he had to sit quietly in classes that he found easy, like German, and not stand out from his classmates.

"SNOW!" James and Jordan cheered. They were planning for the first year snowball fight at lunchtime. Inviting the entire peer group was a must. On break time Melissa had sat across the car park writing in a wire-bound notebook leaning against the silver metal fence which bordered the car park. The cape assembly still gave JW Goosebumps so he found it best to avert his eyes whenever he saw Melissa. Despite this problem, he could guess she was probably sitting there waiting for her classmates to brave the cold to attend Mrs Elliot's hut for Citizenship. Although, Jordan hadn't mentioned having that after break on Tuesday, didn't 1A2 have Science with the "expert" skeleton joker? He frowned, it would not be Melissa was here to stalk him like the rumours...

"Melissa! I know Louise might not want you to but we thought you'd enjoy joining in the snow ball fight at lunch?" Jordan hopped across the tarmac to invite her. The green huts looked less inviting covered in snow, considering they were apparently made of cardboard it was not fun to be inside them in this weather either, they had three mini heaters in each hut and it was still not warm enough compared to inside the main school building, he thought. JW watched his classmates chatting and started to daydream. He remembered back to a few weeks prior, when he had asked Melissa about her friend's argument on the first week of school.

They had been sat in Geography, where James had been begging him to bring his new guitar into school to show them. Melissa had walked in at that point and was meandering her way to her seat when Jordan had come up behind her and tapped her arm.

"You wouldn't believe it but according to Johanna, AJ locked Louise in the girl's bathroom," He had told them all.

"Oh no, I hope she's okay?" Melissa had replied immediately.

"I noticed Chatterbox and John have gone to skive since lunch, must've been their crime that they're avoiding. Will she be ok?" Alisha probed. She had made her way over from beside Angela and the other nice girls to speak to the members of her registration class about the situation.

"Oh man, she's furious! Her Mum's here and she's even more fuming too," Jordan responded. He regarded Melissa who rubbed her arms nervously. She was wearing a long sleeved black shirt with a glittery sequined vest over the top. It looked like 80's or 90's punk fashion but she was adorable... JW remembered, blushing at the memory. He had gathered by then, Jordan was quite concerned for his ex-girlfriend, but not to say he still fancied her, more he cared about her a lot. It was then Melissa revealed other information.

"Yeah, um, you see... Louise has been getting bullied by AJ a bit recently," Melissa admitted. The faces around her washed-out and gasped with brimming curiosity. "So since it's been going on for a while her mum's gotten the police involved. The school's not able to do things cos it's mostly happening outside," she went on. She brushed a hand through her hair making it stick up in a cowlick when she put her hand back down.

"Like what? What's been happening?" Jordan enquired with concern. "My Mum said she'd heard something but it's right vague, you know neighbourhood whispers."

"Ugh, well..." she heaved a heavy sigh. "Like following her home from school and kicking her bag, I didn't think it was so big to involve police, but you know Louise," she mumbled, JW sat behind her leaning against the desk he shared with his own best friend. Perry was sat at his desk watching the conversation with curiosity as it unfolded around them. It was the only channel on and he had exhausted the television remote.

"I wonder when this sub will arrive," he grumbled with boredom examining his nails.

"I don't know," JW flung at him. A few minutes later and the substitute teacher actually did turn up. Then after class JW hung back to pack his things before joining his friends to go to his locker. Since it was the end of the school day on a Wednesday he was going to cycle home for his lesson with Dean. Nevertheless, he was curious when he saw Melissa and Jordan having a chat outside class together. Mostly because she usually walked home with Louise and the other girls, but never with Jordan.

Melissa and Jordan whispered to each other before turning round to face him. "What?" Melissa cooed as she spun on him, smiling. He had been staring at her Hooch trousers again. JW blushed slightly, and made a point of making eye contact.

"N-nothing, um, Melissa?" Jordan gave him a look but muttered to Melissa that he would go see if Louise was still in the school. That explained it, the boy was going to walk home with them to make sure that the girls were safe. That made sense, JW realised.

"You look like you wanted to ask me something?" Melissa asked him then. She relaxed into her cape and body warmer. He felt squeamish walking next to her in the hallway in case someone else saw them alone together. That's not nice, he chastised himself then.

"I was wondering if you could tell me why Louise over reacted the other day when Chatterbox asked about your necklace?" he quizzed, pointing to her chest.

"Oh you mean this?" Melissa replied immediately, casually pulling her pentagram from under her sequined t-shirt.

"Uh-uh yeah," JW stuttered in affirmation as the pentagram necklace in question swung back and forth in front of him.

"I don't know why she reacted that way, since she didn't seem all that interested when I explained it to her. She's more upset about me wearing this tacky rope it's on with the silver friendship necklace she got me for Christmas."

"So there's no chance you're actually a witch?" JW asked her, with a casual laugh. His eyes following the swing of the pentagram.

"Everyone in school has been taking that rumour way too seriously," Melissa complained, rolling her eyes. "Did you know about what happened to me in English on Wednesday last term?"

"Huh? What's that got to do with it?"

"That's a good question, my friend. Anyway, I was researching in the library and Samantha saw I'd looked up Witchcraft, so now I keep getting asked that witch question. It's so dumb," Melissa laughed it off. "I mean, Andrew threw his books at me and chanted *she's a witch* the next time I was in English," she mumbled.

"Y-you're avoiding my question. Ok, so what does your necklace mean?" he queried in a different way, reaching out for it as she held it dangling from her hand. Melissa almost snatched it away protectively, hesitantly, she could tell he meant well. He had put it across in a nice tone so she knew he was merely curious.

"Heh, nothing," she laughed lightly again, letting JW hold the warm pewter pentagram for a moment to examine it.

"Really?"

"It's just a necklace," she lied.

While JW was busy ruminating over his daydream, Jordan invited three girls in total from his registration class to join their snowball fight. Angela and her friend's from his registration class were also joining in, as were some people from other groups. D group and E group were also joining in; this included the ginger Mark who was in their F classes, and most of his friends who had attended the Anderson's primary school together. Despite the fact it had been almost a year the Primary schools still held the same rivalry between them. People would see Applegrove pupils as the most aggressive and least sporting in a fight such as this. JW discussed this topic with Perry over their next two classes. They would be meeting on the Roysvale sports field across from the public swimming pool, which would be big enough and far enough away from the Academy.

"I'm concerned you'll get your coat dirty Mel," Louise told her best friend, as they waited by the locker before going outside. JW was just leaving the boy's toilets to meet James and Jordan to go outside at lunchtime. He hadn't spoken to Louise since the start of school so when he stood beside her had expected a reaction.

"Oh hi JW," she beamed. He greeted her with less enthusiasm and then she turned away from him again.

"Och aye! You're right."

"What, Jordan agreeing with me?" the blonde puffed out of sarcasm. "That's a first," she said mid-cough.

"Yeah, Mel your Dad'll kill me if I let you ruin that designer coat of yours. Why not stash yours in Lulu's locker and borrow one of ours?" Jordan suggested, ignoring his ex-girlfriend's sarcasm and using her childish nickname to annoy her. Her face grew red and she mumbled swearwords. James took that moment to interject.

"Aye, have mine, I'll wear my anorak," James offered, shaking off his oversized blue ski-jacket and holding it out for her.

"You sure you won't be cold?" Melissa gasped, raising her eyebrows. It was endearing how surprised she was at his generosity. She unbuttoned her cape and handed it to Louise who seized it gently, folded it up neatly and hugged it like a newborn baby.

"Course not, the cold doesn't bother me anyway. I have a Satanist heart," He countered thumping his chest.

"Aye! He's a big strong man. No homo," Jordan added after the girls raised their eyebrows.

By the end of lunchtime that day Melissa was indeed not the only one who was glad she had borrowed a coat from someone. At one point JW had smacked a snowball in her face and if she hadn't been wearing a waterproof coat it would have gotten her soaked in the front. He cursed his friend for denying him of being able to see Melissa's clothes get wet but quickly realised she would be more upset about the cape. Later on Mark had slipped a handful of ice down her back so at one point he did get his wish.

The most brutal part of the first year fight happened about halfway through when a guy from the upperclassmen joined in and it became a free for all where they didn't know who was throwing snow at who. He came home battered and bruised but it was the most fun JW had ever had at school. Unfortunately, due to the large scale and the amount of foul play, the teachers promptly issued a warning against future snowball fights. Roysvale and any area nearby Forres Academy would be under stricter supervision until the weather cleared up.

It was near the end of lunch when JW was confused by the turn of events. One minute he was watching Melissa shaking off snow from the back of the coat James had lent her. The next, she had vanished in a whisper of blue light before his eyes.

"Did you see where Melissa went? She still has my coat?" the tall boy snivelled shivering. Jordan was also soaked through from the waist down. The three boys looked around and saw people were filtering away from Roysvale and the girls were all gone.

"Group hug?" he asked, and they laughed joyfully.

"Yes, please," JW replied his teeth chattering. Conveniently disremembering the disappearing act as a trick...

Chapter Eleven

It had been a calm morning after a night of excitement and Melinda was being driven home from school at the Steiner school in the afternoon. Yesterday had been a Pagan holiday and the Coven had celebrated it all together. Imbolc, the celebration of rebirth and fertility. It was often confused with Candlemas, as it involved a lot of candles... although, is the Christian holiday commemorating the presentation of Jesus at the Temple. It falls on February 2, Imbolc honours the Celtic Goddess Brigid, and is a Gaelic traditional festival marking the beginning of spring. Quentin stopped in the Spar to refuel his '98 Golf.

"Want anything from the shop?" He asked her, politely.

"Surprise me," Melinda wagered, shrugging off her belt as she relaxed in the passenger seat. She watched as Quentin marched into the shop and slowly made his way to the cash register, perusing the aisles as he did. The car engine created steam in the mixture of temperatures. The car was warm. She adored the snow but it was always nicer to be inside on a day like this. She thought about what her younger sister, Alison, was up to after school- probably making snow angels in the playground in front of Alves Primary School. Her Mum, Marlene, was most likely already home preparing for the girls to make their way there. Hopefully getting ready to meet them all with delicious and luxurious homemade hot chocolate... with marshmallows, whipped cream and Cadbury flakes. Melinda felt her mouth just watering at the thought.

"I wonder if he has any music," she said out loud, rifling through the compartments of his dashboard. The doors were empty of most things irrelevant to the car's maintenance so she thought he'd have something tucked away. Luckily there were a few CD's in the glove compartment. Had she not been weary of it she might have ignored the strange book hidden under the Great British road map as it drew her attention then. In alarm she noticed it was his Book of Shadows. Ignoring the book blessing inside the first page she flicked through, looking for a date that was marked. The entire diary was written in the Wiccan language, Theban. Other letters she recognised throughout; Ancient Futhark, Latin, Welsh and a few were even Tolkien scripts. This date in question was written in Theban, which Melinda could translate with ease because it was a code she had learnt from her parents ever since she could learn to read and write. She skimmed the page and felt a sick feeling in her stomach. She read what she could quickly and then put the book back where she found it...

July 17 2001

Today I travelled with Melinda Barnes to view the woods and hills of Glen Tanar, her favourite place in Scotland. She is fourteen and I am seventeen, but Melinda looks much older, as if she could be sixteen or seventeen. She matured quickly. Her skin is the colour of honey with a few hundred freckles and her hair is a mahogany brown with delicate ringlets.

When I pulled over my Golf I explained this to her, and I leant over from the driver's seat. "What are you doing?" she asked in shock. I was close enough to see the puckering of her t-shirt and cardigan. She trusted me to such an extent she did not wear a bra. "Car trouble" I mumbled and excused myself reluctantly from the car to go look at the engine. As I muttered to myself and forced open the front of my car I could see what the issue was. The two poppets were now tied loosely together. They must have fallen undone in the last speed bump. I secured them together tightly and then put both back in the space between the engine and the bottom of the car. I wiped my hands on my jeans before I closed the front bonnet again. She smiled warmly at me as I slid back into the driver's seat. Her eyes now sang with my appraisal.

"All better?" She asked, of course, meaning the car. I nodded and closed the driver's side door. She slid her arms around me then and we admired the world outside in each other's company. This woods was a place gave her spiritual enlightening and feelings of being surrounded by Mother Earth. It was her sacred place, she explained in great detail to me. She visited it very often growing up in Scotland, more than the other idyllic hiking locations.

"Would you kiss me?" she asked suddenly, I thought about this as being a direct conclusion to how tightly I had bound the poppets. The one poppet that looked like me with my Wiccan & Coven name. The other looked like her, with her name- since she had told me it.

We are childhood friends, we grew up together. I had lived near her and my family were part of her coven until my cousin Kelsey was born and my Mum had decided we had to move back to Wales to be with her sister and other relatives there. I was born in Wales, so I felt a belonging to there, but my father had always been part of the coven in Ayrshire, Scotland. This now, I am invited as a guest of the Barnes' to watch my friend Melinda become an even more powerful Witch- at Lammas when she is initiated fully into the coven. Her goal is to eventually become the High Priestess of her own coven and train other young powerful girls.

"We have been friends so long and you make me feel so safe. Would you please kiss me?" she said now, and I did more than just that. I seduced her in my own car. She smiled up at me as I came...

Melinda couldn't bear to read any more as it made the bile rise in her throat. The rest was graphic and the details were things she couldn't remember. She tried hard to remember that, but it gave her a headache to try. She truthfully *did* know they had gone to Glen Tanar, as it was an annual event before Lammas for her. The sick feeling was still there as Quentin returned from the Spar and flopped down into his car.

"I bet your Ma has her delicious hot chocolate ready for us. Good thing too, it's fucking freezing, my hands are so cold. Get your seat belt back on," he ordered as he turned on the ignition and the engine roared to life. Melinda considered the poppets under the car bonnet and how they connected to her headache. They are meant to heal people, she thought angrily.

"Hmm, yeah," she nodded, obediently connecting in her seat belt again. She wondered what Quentin would do if she ran away from him then.

Chapter Twelve

I'm not late. Who am I kidding school's miles away and I've got to be there in five minutes; thought Melissa as she crossed the street on her way to school. She was so distracted by her own thoughts she did not notice what was coming until a neighbour yelled her name from the other side of the road. A lorry was coming straight at her. She was so stunned she could not think; just raised her hands up in defence. She thought about two different things at once; not sure how fast she could manage to get off the road in time and leg it to school as well. In one way she wanted to tell the lorry and the world around her to stop. There was the conflict of the previous thoughts about getting to school as quickly as possible. Then she was gone – in a blue light. Gosh that could have been a devastating slip up if the witnesses had been wide awake. Assuming they must had ONLY imagined she had been standing in the middle of the road.

"If I hadn't heard him I would have been road kill!" she told herself shivering. Melissa appeared in an empty hallway next to a green door. Wait what did I just do? She asked herself moments later. Had she done that thing again? The one her Auntie Anne did when she moved from the closet to the attic and back within seconds. What was it called? Something in Latin. Melissa gasped. She looked through the glass panels on the door and saw two girls standing at a set of lockers on the left hand side. The girl in front was Jenny, a rather nasty girl, the other was Samantha, Jenny's girlfriend, a girl who Melissa was not particularly fond of either. Melissa opened the door slightly and pushed her hand through. Palm opened out and twisted it a little; the whole corridor froze.

Tempus rerum imperator; she thought, willing the time to slow so she could sneak past the girls and go to her registration class. This one she knew quite well. Melissa smiled smugly as she turned to walk towards the English corridor where her classmates would be.

On the way into her registration she bumped into Chloe and Corey Black. Corey was taller than both girls now since he had turned twelve and had a tiny growth spurt, and his short blonde hair on top of his black school clothes making him resemble a young James Bond. Chloe had sleek black hair, a red schoolbag and a blue jumper. They chatted a little but Melissa did not like the feeling of being a third wheel, nope, so she ended the conversation rather abruptly before it ran away with itself. Melissa pondered this. She was different not just because she was a witch but also because she was a tom-boy: she hated to wear things like skirts and makeup, talking about kissing boys and all the positively girly things like that, which is what Chloe and the other girls wanted to talk about. Then the subject of JW came up; they were talking about something he had taken into school and was showing off to his friends outside. The girls giggled. The boys table on the other side of the room were busy with their own conversation. The registration teacher was engaging with the boys because they liked to exchange banter after she had finished marking off names. The morning radio played in the background. With all this noise around her Melissa's heart beat was the loudest thing in her ears and for a moment she held on to the thought. She blushed deeply and swallowed hard.

"I don't know where that came from," Melissa mumbled, thinking out loud. She had a horrible thought maybe she hadn't appeared alone in the corridor a few moments ago, but JW had walked by behind her and he had gone into the boys toilets with something shiny in his hand.

"Where what came from?" Alisha wondered, looking at her classmates, Chloe and Johanna, and they all turned towards Melissa with muddled looks.

"Melissa are you okay?" Johanna asked, realising that Melissa was zoning out and staring at her face with intense concern. Melissa nodded, aware they were fretful that she might faint and so did her best to reassure them. The gaggle of girls proceeded with their conversation, ignoring her again but to her relief also leading the topic away from JW.

"JW's playing with a lightsabre in class, what a nerd!" Josh Cole squealed laughing. Jenny and Samantha echoed him;
"Nerd!"
This was how it started while Mr Nellany was out of the room. Melissa turned around and looked at her crush as he slumped his head on the desk. She had been so happy the day they had been placed into seats so close to each other; until he borrowed her purple pencil sharpener and was reluctant to return it, which had made her incredibly sad.

"Oh he's crying!" Samantha shouted, which made them laugh harder and chant more. Even Perry and Jordan, who had joined in with making fun of him, despite having been friends with JW, carried on. To them it was funny. Melissa realised, with a dull sensation, she was the only person in the class who did not find "taking the piss" out of a classmate even remotely funny... what sick human beings they were, she thought.

"I hate this class," she heard JW whimpering from under his arms. She could see tears in his sea-green eyes if she looked up from under the desk; which of course made him swear at her to "Fucking leave me alone!" before he stomped out of class to get Mr Nellany.

"That's enough!" The laidback teacher sighed as he entered the classroom. JW did not return for the rest of class. Naturally, Melissa sought out her crush before their next class, Mathematics.

"JW are you ok?" she queried with concern as she cornered him in the alcove beside reprographics. He had been sat down in the small seated area where students were sent if they felt sick during classes and had to wait for parents to collect them. The noise of the photocopier in the room behind them beeped as JW raised slowly from his seat. The wine-red walls and linoleum reflecting his feelings as he snapped his toy lightsaber in two. Red plastic clattered on the floor and he swung the hilt towards her neck.

"What part of fucking leave me alone did you not get?"

"S-sorry..." she mumbled, tears building in her eyes. She cowered away from him then and did the best thing she could think of out of fear. "Tempus Motus," she hissed biting back tears, they weren't listening to her as she tried to command the big pools of salty liquid to stop. There, even though she knew it was a weapon, she was crying. "Tempus motus..." she wailed again.

"Stop it," JW snarled grabbing her hand and dropping his broken toy. "If you cry in school it'll just embarrass us both," he reasoned, his voice hoarse and uncaring.

"B-but, y-you c-c-ried too!" she blubbered, he had quite a firm grip on her wrist then and she was nervous about what might happen next. People were walking past them without as much as a look in from the sea of students and teachers out in the busy corridor.

"You're right," JW realised, his eyes growing wide. He slackened his grip enough for Melissa to pull her wrist free. JW looked at his hand, had he actually been that angry? He softened his face and looked at her with something akin to pity. I'm sorry, he thought, but the words were caught in his throat. Melissa stepped away and was consumed into the crowd of students.

"I should have known better than to check on him," Melissa told herself as she made her way into her mathematics class where Mrs Riddoch magically knew already where she had been.

*

The next day Melissa was walking to school. This time she had woken up early enough to be able to walk the entire distance, rather than cheating and using her *tempus motus momentum* ability, as she thought it was called. Taking the way to school where she had to cross Orchard road and walk down St Catherine's road to Fleur's place instead of walking with Louise like before. She did this to try to catch a glimpse of JW- it made her feel safer when she was out on her own.

It was then she felt a crackle in the air. It felt like Deja vu, she felt as if she had paused by the fence between the bins and entrance to the play park like this before. That was when she turned around and saw Perry and JW walking towards –

– the world went into slow motion. Her heart beat stopped for a moment and then her sight was blocked by a premonition; Perry was asking me out, not for himself but for JW, and they were sat in English next to me –

Melissa blanched and toppled back into the fence post for support. Her eyes went back into focus and James was standing in front of her making chimpanzee noises and bouncing around on his toes. JW laughed, a touch of monkey glee to his musical chortle; and Perry laughed, which was like a hyenas laugh; and another boy who was standing across the street was laughing too until a pair of skinny legged older girls took his interest and he slithered after them. Melissa blushed and hid behind her straight, black hair, which grew to shoulder length. JW's gorgeous, greyish-green eyes searched her brown eyes, with a look of concern. She quickly turned and carried on with her morning walk to school, blushing deeper.

Several hours and four periods later, it was Friday lunchtime, and Melissa was sitting alone at her favourite spot in the whole of school: the silver metal fence overlooking the car park at the back of school. It was the best place where she could be secluded and able to write or read at her leisure. She did not have many friends in school but the ones who did joined her, occasionally, ate their lunch at this spot. There was another reason she liked it: she could watch her crush saunter past in his tight trousers.

JW and his friends were walking past her to the little football pitch just behind the trees, while she was busily writing in her Book of Shadows, she glanced up but made certain he was unaware of her gaze. As if he was instead the psychic one, or had felt her lingering gaze on his back, JW spun on his heel abruptly. He came up to her and started mumbling.

"Oh, how's it going?" She asked nonchalantly, raising her face to give him her full attention. He cleared his throat. Her bright smile fell away slowly.

"This is going to sound really hella weird, but you have to know that thing is a joke, so don't take it seriously. Got it?"

"I'm weird 24-7," was her sharp reply, obviously disappointed in the lack of friendly conversation. Honestly, how rude could he be? He nodded and backed away. Melissa's mind bumbled with possibilities and she blushed so much she worried about walking into her next class with the blush there permanently...

At the end of Music, Perry came up to Melissa, who had thankfully not been blushing for an entire period, and asked if she would walk to English with him. She felt goaded into it but at the same time it was only logical they walk together as they also sat together in their English class. After they had entered Mrs Brown's first year English classroom they sat down at their table by the window. She showed no reaction as the dark haired, spotty boy with glasses leaned towards her- at first she thought he might have dropped something- but he leant right up to her and dropped a scrap of paper in her lap.

Will you go out with JW?

"I guess there's more morbid fairy stuff today," He hissed, a smirk on his pearly white teeth and then he resumed gathering his jotter and pencil case without another word. She considered the premonition for the longest time possible, refusing to allow herself a look over at where her crush was sat. Unlike her vision, he *was not* sat at the desk on the other side of Perry. It was different, she thought, but not unusual. Then she thought, in the premonition she had heard Perry say the words "Will you go out with JW?" It was not a note... her stomach contorted into knots and she felt queasy.

"Um, yeah," she shrugged, swallowing hard, uncurling the note under the table. Melissa wrote her reply on the paper and immediately slipped it back to him. Once she was sure he had seen it she inhaled and exhaled deeply. Melissa remembered her premonition and thought it would be good if she said yes... but then realised moments later was a terribly wrong choice, as in their English class a number of people were already laughing at her, most were literally behind her back.

"She SAID yes? What a weirdo!" Samantha gasped a bit too loudly as Mrs Brown waddled into class with a box full of English books from the story Skellig which they had been reading as a class.

"Really, she likes the Dutch boy? But he's such a wimp!" Jenny added, as if to confirm the subject matter. A torrential heckling filled the room as Mrs Brown set to work on preparing the board for the afternoon's lesson, ignoring the back rows. Despite this embarrassment, Melissa felt rather daring as she glanced over at JW where he sat near the far wall behind his friends James and Jordan.

He simply hit his head on his desk with a loud thump.

"Did you say yes?" JW asked Melissa in shock, as they ambled along the dirt path near to the river Mosset on the way home. They walked side by side with their school bags on their backs. JW wore his over one shoulder with his green winter coat zipped all the way up to protect from the chill.

"No!" she spat immediately, blushing. Just then Jenny and Samantha walked up behind her holding hands.

"WOO-WOO!" they wailed, imitating a police car.

"You dork's are cute," Jenny snarled.

"I can be so stupid sometimes!" She heard JW mutter through gritted teeth as he marched ahead, trying to put as much distance between them as his stocky legs could manage. That's what I was thinking, Melissa thought glumly, I'm so stupid, and you should hate me. As she strode onwards the two taller girls followed her, making their noises and laughing, oblivious to the fact they were being ignored. The two girls stalked her until the dark green bridge where they crossed the river to go up towards the Crescent and Melissa continued on the same path.

"What happened?" Louise Owens asked, bluntly, meeting her best friend at the end of Burdshaugh road... who was in tears and muttering incoherently while they crossed the busy road.

"Well you know that premonition I told you about when I met you at break earlier?" Melissa managed to say eventually after she had calmed down a bit. She had been handed a tissue by a friendly stranger, a woman walking her dog in the afternoon, who looked at both the young girls with concern. The woman gave over the tissue while her dog yipped and jumped about the girl's legs excitedly. Dogs are the best medicine, Louise thought when the friendly dog walker left them, and smiled as she walked away. She sighed with annoyance and turned to her friend.

"What?" she hissed angrily, snapping from one mood to another faster than the flick of a light switch, and smacking her friend in the shoulder. "You're so stupid and confused that you think you have magic powers! It was just a dream stop going on about it. Would you just cheer up, you're such an embarrassment," Louise grumbled.

"I know, JW just told me that too!" Melissa hissed back angry with her for not listening.

"JW?" she muttered, shaking her head and, catching sight of her younger cousin David, turned to greet him with a wave as he cycled towards them. I wish Melissa would get over her crush on JW, Louise thought as she watched her cousin, who was still a pupil in Applegrove Primary school, dismount and join them on the pavement. They exchanged stories of their day as they walked home, Melissa was quiet, but it was nothing unusual. Then, to Louise and David's obvious surprise, she spoke up.

"Why would he have told me it was a joke if he didn't like me just a tiny bit?" Melissa thought out loud, mumbling, but loud enough for the two Owens's to hear her. "I don't know why I said that, because he probably started laughing about the whole thing being a joke as soon as he was away from me."

144

"How could you say that? He likes you a lot, otherwise he wouldn't talk to you at all," Louise replied, incredulously. Of course, she knew Melissa would ignore her like always.

"I think he hates me and I prefer that. If I allow myself to wonder otherwise my stupid girly mind will become hopelessly convinced he will ask me out one day and mean it. So I can't ask him out; I don't ask him out or talk to him and everyone will eventually leave me alone and stop picking on me. That's how I'd write this, in my Book of shadows, and I will do as soon as I get home," Melissa sighed at the end of her external monologue. The red haired children stood with their mouths open in shock. David dropped his bike and Louise, who was usually emotionally violent, looked at her friend with warmth. She slid the straps off her school bag, threw her bag on the ground and brought her arms wide while she took a step towards Melissa- who backed away tearfully.

"I want to hug you, you idiot. David, be a man and hug her too," Louise ordered, and he did as his older cousin demanded. That was how Melissa had the first group hug in her entire life.

Chapter Thirteen

The hall door was slammed shut with a loud bang and a groaning sound. A classic signature of any grumpy teenager, if there ever was no other way to make an entrance they knew how.

"Melissa, are you alright?" Richard asked his daughter as she stomped into the living room that afternoon. David and Louise Owens, although they had meant well, were not fully equipped to aid her in her plight. Richard could sense this all once his daughter approached him then; additionally, he had seen her outside the window with their neighbour and her younger cousin.

"I'm fine, Da!" the teenager moaned in reply as she fell onto the armrest and then flopped backwards. She removed her school shoes and then curled up in front of the television.

"Have you had any other premonitions? You can talk to me about interpreting them if you like. Or if it's something else, I can try to get a long distance call up. I don't mind being offline for a while," he suggested, referring to his sister in America.

"Eh, no Dad, it's not *that*! I did say I'm fine," she insisted, covering her head with a throw cushion.

"How are you faring with learning from those books we got you for your Birthday?" he enquired, sighing from frustration and leaning towards her from his armchair. Single parenting was annoying, without his sister around to help he was at a loss. He had female friends helped a lot, like Louise's family, but they knew nothing about the other occurrences.

"Good, fine," Richard could hear her say from under the purple velvet cushion. She was being so frustrating today, he thought.

"Have you been using any temporal-you-knows-what's?" he added awkwardly, his nerves apparent. Melissa was showing a lot of promise for her young age and that was daunting.

"Umm, I think I'll go upstairs," Melissa mumbled hesitantly forcing herself from the comfy furniture and flinging the cushion across the room at the same time.

"Oh, ok, be down for dinner. Remember Louise is coming over tonight to stay for the weekend. She's bringing her Mum's homemade chicken hot pot," he added hoping it would encourage her to come back downstairs to eat.

"I'll be back in a bit for a cup of tea," she called down to ease his mind. Richard rolled his eyes and focussed his attention on the other drama playing out on the television.

"Help ma bob," he whispered to himself, allowing a small smile. He relaxed into his armchair again, resting his elbow on the armrest and holding his stubbly chin in his hand.

*

A couple of hours later Louise was in the Galloway house. Upstairs in Melissa's bedroom she had her overnight bag, her straighteners and her favourite pillow from home- it had the warm smell of dog on it.

"So my parents are both away for the weekend. My Dad rented them a hotel in the big city while they take my brother to visit Saint Andrew's university."

"Okay, well, I suppose it'll work out like last time you were left with us when you were younger," Richard Galloway responded. He ate rather fast between mouthfuls, he enjoyed home cooked meals and this was in a way his payment for babysitting and pet-sitting.

"Huh?" Louise mumbled, her mouth full of chicken and roast potatoes. "You know I don't remember," she continued after swallowing her food.

"Yeah, you stayed for sleeping and eating here but we went back to your place to see the dogs three times a day," Melissa's Dad prompted her. "I remember it well," he nodded. The early memories like those when Melissa was younger were important, as memories of their own children were to any father.

"Oh yeah I was like, I don't know, seven!" Louise gasped.

"Eight, deffo eight! You only got Jess that year," Richard added, he sat with an empty plate in front of him while the girls were still working on their meals.

"She was the cutest puppy," Louise cooed, "so full of energy! So playful! She would always rough house with the rest of the puppies from her litter."

"I thought she was crazy," Melissa injected into the conversation. She had barely spoken all evening, yet her father and best friend were more concerned she ate her meal. It was an odd dynamic they shared, almost like Louise was a stand-in or a step-mother.

"Shush! Eat your greens," she wanted to say, cringing inwardly. She looked down at their two plates. In order to feel comfortable she chewed her food slowly, but Melissa, now, she full on played with her food. Turtles and tortoises moved faster than her, but then, they do like vegetables (especially cabbages).

"Mel, come on, if you want to talk about crazy dogs just remember the one from the litter my Aunt Beatrix adopted?" Louise said instead, wiping her face as she noticed gravy had dribbled from her mouth. She knew she would have to reapply her lip gloss after dessert. They were having rhubarb crumble with ice cream. Not that it was important to the plot, just that they would have that after their chicken hot pot.

"Excuse me, I'll just get the pudding and reheat it in the microwave," Richard perked up quickly, as if the rhubarb was beckoning him.

"Ok, well," Louise smiled at her friend's Dad. She placed her cutlery side-by-side like she would in a restaurant and then continued on with the conversation. "I think that dog was totally a lesbian! It is still like she doesn't even know that Jess is her sister. Dogs certainly are funny," Louise giggled. Melissa joined in on the joke. Richard looked at them both, he gave a curious smile as he carried over the serving dish.

"Okay, are you both done now or would you like seconds?"

"Nah, just ice cream and pudding please," Louise replied politely, she craned her neck to look at the microwave as it was opened, beeping away the seconds when it was closed behind her. This part of the day was considerably quiet, she thought, and if she had been at home it would be spent loading up the dish washer. Her

Mum was super against junk food, because she had to maintain her father's cholesterol, dessert was something they saved for special occasions. Certain older brothers going away to universities where Princes' attended was an astoundingly special occasion for the Owens' – Louise reminded herself – she had been slightly shocked he had been accepted. It was a righteously prestigious school, so he was a lucky older brother, and she knew she was meant to be proud of him. However, her thoughts were laden with sarcasm and more than just a normal hint of jealousy.

"Melissa?" Richard prodded. Bringing the redhead from her reverie so that she looked up at the brunette. "Are you finished with your potatoes?"

"Yeah, Mel, they're had enough of your tomfoolery."

"Oh ha-ha!" Melissa stuck out her clean tongue with a cheeky grin. Louise was glad she had successfully made her smile finally.

"What's got your goat?" she asked her after dessert when they were upstairs in her room.

"Nothing new," Melissa sighed.

"Come on! JW's not gonnae ask himself out, now, is he?" Louise remarked, rolling her eyes. They were laid out on her bed after eating and were reading a book. Richard had let himself out to go walk Jess and Tara, to allow the girl's time to work on their homework, apparently. In fact he just wanted an excuse to see the dogs- he couldn't have any because of his heavy work life and being a single father.

"Ugh, instead of answering your question how about I go do my chores. Dishes aren't gonnae do themselves either..." Melissa hissed in an acidic tone.

"Ooh, touchy, take a chill pill. I've got to reapply my make-up, anyhoo," she grumbled in a similar tone.

"Figures," Melissa tutted, rolling her eyes again. There was enough attitude and tension in the room to fuel a civil war.

"Go on then," Louise huffed, busying herself by looking through her overnight bag while Melissa stood up and strode from the room. When she heard her best friend taking a strop down the stairs she moved from her own bag to the school bag beside it which belonged to Melissa. It was sat leaning against her wooden night stand, lying open, with a rather tempting looking wire-bound notebook...

12th ~~Februbery~~ February 2002

When me and Louise were at my house after school today we had my dad's old cauldron out, really it was a heat proof bronze shaded bowl used for potion making. She was doing a little spell to increase her memory, to put it clear she was cheating for a test she had in history. She don't take Wicca seriously, to her it's a joke. Her auntie is a grey witch and tells her different thing to how my Da and my Aunt sais.

Louise had left and I was doing the true love spell I looked in the cauldron and as I looked back at the parchment something had made a strange shape, no not a shape letters two letters, J and W it was odd, really he hates me, right? - MG

152

Louise flicked through the pages until she found the latest entry:-

22ⁿᵈ February

I had a vision where I was in my English class when I laughed about a thing being a joke and the girl, Bill J. she has black hair and round glasses like Perry's, he sat beside JW and Jordan behind me. But that hasn't happened. That wasn't how it happened. So I must be getting visions of the future when this stuff will happen again. I want to ask my Da about it cos he gets visions too but I'm scared cos he might say I'm misusing my powers. Da wants me to learn for myself so I can find my own path. Black is bad hand path, grey is in-betweeny. I want to be white. - MG

Louise was borderline fuming, so she would say. What did that all mean? She had glanced over the True Love spell and only saw a description about rose oil and pink candles. It was bizarre but boring. The stuff about her though, was the problem. Louise allowed herself to calm down and hurriedly put away her friend's diary. She had never spoken to Melissa about the things her aunt had taught her being "Grey" she had thought of it as being harmless fun. It just was not real, to her it was like what they always watched on TV. Just teenage girls pretending to be witches.

"Hey, may I help you?" Melissa spat, appearing abruptly. There was a displacement in the air as if she had brought with her a whoosh of heat from the kitchen.

"W-h-hat the f-u-c-k, I didn't even hear you come up!" Louise stuttered, stumbling back onto the bed. She went a ghostly white colour made her freckles stand out even more.

"There's a good reason," Melissa chuckled, sitting on the bed. She felt excited, but in a way knew she did something wrong a second later when her temples knotted into a migraine. "Ouch."

"Ouch?" Louise repeated dumbfounded, eyebrows raised.

"I thought you were supposed to be putting on. Make-up?" She just about managed to say, the tightness around her head and mind increasing. Melissa rubbed her forehead and fell next to her friend on the bed. She felt awfully tired, due to her brain being overworked, and had to lie down before she fainted from the mental exhaustion.

"Oh yeah," Louise found it unexpectedly dreadfully difficult to come up with a convincing enough lie. Instead, in her panic, she admitted to reading the Book of Shadows.

Chapter Fourteen

School started out as ordinary again the following Monday. The mood was calm throughout the morning with Melissa spending time with her friends from registration at break before they separated for mathematics afterwards. Things were tense during fourth period German class. Perry and JW kept their heads together and did not talk to anyone aside from the teacher or each other. Meanwhile Melissa struggled to ignore the sniggering behind her back while at the same time focusing on listening to their teacher.

Then at lunch, at the back of the school, Melissa sat at her thinking spot and read a book. There was some third years and other boys trying to pick a fight with JW nearby so she watched from a distance as they argued. He ran out of the school grounds across the road and up into the woods. Melissa stealthily followed him in the shadows until he disappeared. She ducked down, to avoid the gang of smokers, and then heard two boy's asking one of the gang of where JW had gone. It took her a moment to realise the two boys were James and Jordan, her classmates, who were trying to find JW out of concern. She followed them.

"Hey, girl, want to hang out with us? You can have some fags if you like?" AJ offered her the open packet, giving a friendly smirk, as Melissa was a girl in her registration class- when AJ ever went to school before noon. Melissa mumbled a polite decline in reply and then crept after the two boys, not truly saying goodbye to her older classmate. AJ shrugged and resumed talking to her gang. Melissa circled around Sanquhar woods but she could not find JW and had also lost track of the other two boys from her class. Then, when she did manage to get down onto the main foot path again, to go back towards the school, James marked her and took long strides to meet her. Startled by being spotted she froze on the spot.

"Hey, we've just seen JW walking through the car park. The third years've gotten bored so they've left," James told her, Melissa nodded but was afraid of saying anything in case he made fun of her. James meant well but because of his height and his abundance of confidence she found him intimidating. "If you want to speak to him," James added, grinning. Melissa kept her head down and walked away from her classmate, again not saying anything to him. She ambled back towards the school where she saw JW was sitting on the patch of grass across from her silver fence. He had his head in his hands and was kneeling. She ignored the butterflies in her stomach and knelt beside him.

"Are you alright?" she whispered in the air. He mumbled through his arms but she could not hear the answer. She folded her arms to mimic his sitting position on the wet grass. She thought about what kind of thing she could do; if she were upset like this he might try to make her laugh, but she was not good at making jokes or puns. For a couple minutes they sat there in awkward silence, where she felt uncertain about how he felt about her and wondered when he might speak to her again. Melissa thought about her spells, my "spell to help *a friend in need" might work*, opening her school bag. Extracted her Book of Shadows out of the bag and zipped it up again. She flicked through it, deliberately skipping the true love spell as she came across it, and felt the unusual sensation of déjà vu like she had on Friday morning before school. This situation seemed like the best opportunity to be alone with him but she dared not to ask him out just then, like Louise had so kindly suggested. She felt it would be inappropriate to do so, and feared rejection, so she did her best to forget about it. She could see JW raising his head to look up. She had a sinking feeling about what he was about to say to her. And the bell rang to remind them they had to go inside for their English class with Mrs Brown.

"Melissa, why?" He mouthed to her, seconds before he saw his friends shouting at them to hurry up. They ran across the grass down to the concrete and gravel. From there they joined the bustle of school students who were filtering into the school. They did not speak again for the rest of the day.

The next day Louise had received the results of her history test, which as a first year still was not such a big deal to fail. Although, with her arrogance, she had the pressure of being a beautiful girl with brains, this was a big deal.

"Well, don't blame me for your test results..." Melissa began, attempting to berate her best friend for being naïve. "You know this isn't how any of it works. I told you on the day you cheated for the test. I told you again, and again, even more recently on Sunday before you tried to curse Craig into having a broken leg. You can ask the universe for guidance but you cannot rely on the universe alone.

You're only using Magick for your own good, harmful means, so in a way it's your own fault for misusing the craft that you would fail your test that you used Magick to cheat for. It's like Karma, the Rule of Three, it's the main Wiccan law," She looked up at her face and could see that she was not listening at all.

"Seriously, that's what you're goin'tae say?" Louise asked her best friend after revealing the results of her history test to her. Melissa had spent the first five minutes after meeting her friend muttering about how it was her own fault for misusing "Magick".

"To pass a test you gotta study," Louise thought out loud with a condescending tone. "More like another example of how this stuff is a joke!" she shouted, thrusting her fists in the air out of exasperation. Her face was red and her exploitations caused a group of teenage passer-by's to scarper. A murmuration dispersed from the trees like a swarm of bees, as if frightened by a predator. Ancient civilizations that rose and fell in the fertile-crescent would be outcast in by Louise's anger as if she were a would-be Roman Emperor.

"Yes, because-," Melissa resumed, as if to continue her point from before. She sat up on her elbows on the grass but was cut short by her friend interrupting her.

"It don't matter, Mel, just have lunch by yourself, I'm off to the chippy!" Louise fumed, and then turned with a melodramatic swoosh of her rust coloured hair and stomped off.

She decided to go for a walk around the school to pound off her frustration and to prepare herself for her second Physical Education class that week. They were doing laps around Sanquhar woods so she made sure to practice the route they would take, careful not to disturb any wanderers walking their dogs at lunchtime. When she was done memorising the paths Melissa assumed a position by the bike cages.

When JW eventually returned from his lunch Melissa quickly hid behind the wall of the school building beside the fire escape for the technical department that was on the Southeast exit from the school's main building. While JW locked up his bike in the bike cages he chatted casually to his tall red haired friend James. They came towards her to walk towards the gym at the back of the school.

"Gosh, what was that rumbling sound? Mel!?" JW blushed furiously when he crashed into her with his friend. The *rumbling* he was referencing was her pathetic stomach grumble.

"Geez, Mel, was one batch of chips not enough? Your tank clearly is unsatisfied, greedy tum," James joked giving her a small punch in the arm. The two boys carried on walking around the building expecting her to keep pace.

"Are you coming?" They asked, but she was too embarrassed by her stomach complaining to follow them just yet.

"Here, eat a snickers," the redhead offered, and the Dutch boy gave her a shy half-smile. This caused Melissa's butterflies to stir, although they were conflicted by their hunger pang. She grabbed the chocolate bar and opened it with her teeth.

"Woah, careful there Matey, she bites," the other boy said with a wink, she blushed again. Her crush giving her attention made her brain melt. She almost wished it was a co-ed changing room as they went inside to line up outside their separate rooms.

As if aware the author had consistently forgotten to write about them, the two popular girls awaited Melissa in the Girl's changing room. Jenny and Samantha were dressed in just their bra and panties, midway through changing into their kit, when Melissa walked in. She still carried her blush as she glanced over them both. Other girls in their class were hurrying to cover themselves until the door was swung shut- in case there was any boys peeping in at them from the corridor. Melissa rushed into the dry shower cubicles to change. She hated looking at the other girls in her class, it made her realise the negatives of a co-ed changing room. If JW or any boy looked at those two athletic popular girls they would not give her a second glance. As she stripped off her brown Hooch trousers Melissa looked down at her chubby white legs with their stubbly ginger hairs that covered every area from her ankles to her chunky thighs. She looked at her stomach with dismay, if only it was as flat as her classmates, the thought came to her more often than she liked. They were probably making fun of her for hiding while getting changed. With a sigh Melissa put on her gym clothes.

"Hey! Bubble butt!" Jordan shouted when he caught sight of Melissa in the waiting area outside where the class was being herded through a gap in the school huts to go through the car park.

"It's freezing!" a couple of their classmates complained.

"You'll warm up when you get walking and jogging," the teacher reminded them, heading the group along the school grounds.

"Bubble butt?" She heard Jenny cackling. The popular girls smacked her ass in turn and commented on how much it jiggled as they walked towards Sanquhar as a class. Melissa was mortified and her stomach whined. She covered her body parts as she walked through the car park.

"Alright class settle down," the teacher ordered once the entire class were at the start of a fork in the footpath at the top of a hill along from the Sanquhar loch. "I want you to be aware this is outside school grounds so there will be normal members of the public about. I know I've said this countless times since you started first year but there's still some of you that don't quite get the idea."

"No guesses who," Perry, who was dressed as per usual in shorts and a vest despite the weather, said loud enough for the whole class to hear. He looked at Andrew and others in his friend group. Jenny and the other popular girls sniggered. The troublemakers glared in reply.

"Enough chatting, let's get moving," one of Angela's redheaded friends said, her teeth chattering. The girls were all covering up their chests and hugging themselves for warmth. It was times like this Melissa was glad of the padding on her push-up bra. While everyone else was cold there was that padding that she had as a bonus. Although, it didn't help with jogging and she had to deal with boys like Jordan staring sometimes.

"Lovely day isn't it?" Angela said to Melissa as they took off at a jogging pace together. The two tall redheads, Mark and James, were off at a sprint the second the teacher let them all go, competitive against each other. They were followed by the athletic kids who were in top physical condition. This was Perry and his swimming friends and Jenny, Samantha and the other gymnastics and volleyball players. The mid-slow takers who were more busy chatting were pacing themselves around the middle while the least healthy group, the smokers, were constantly monitored by the teacher so they did not run off and set fire to things or whatever they did...

"Yeah," Melissa replied to her classmate after considering the question. She admired the colours in the sky, the weather was clear and had a brisk chill to it, and the sun was low in the sky. As it was approaching Spring-time the sun was setting later than it had been, creating an array of purples and blues against the few gossamer clouds. Soon would be British Summer time when the clocks would change forward an hour. The wildlife too would soon be flocking back to bed in the springtime. This was leading up to the time where signets would be viewable in under a month so long as the weather didn't turn icy again.

"Wow!" she responded, unable to say much more as they reached a steeper incline. The trees were lower here as they approached and the path was uneven.

"Did you look at that mark back there?" Angela asked as she slowed down to watch her footing on the other side of the hilly path.

"No, what do you mean?" Melissa asked, careful not to trip on a rock as they jogged. She had a stitch in her left side that hurt and made her stomach cry out in pain.

"Probably from a Husky or Alsatian. You'll see it next time we go round," the girl added picking up pace again once they had made it down the hill. As they jogged they eventually met up with the other classmates who were at the front. The most competitive of the boys were already tired and out of breathe. They were sweating and swearing. Melissa grabbed her sides as she made it to the end of the path where Jordan was leaning against a tree stump with his friends.

"I think it was a massive beast," they speculated. "Probably big foot or a yeti or whatever," Jordan confessed with excitement.

"Oh come on!" Jenny and Samantha rolled their eyes. The rest of the class shared a similar reaction of disbelief.

"No, get a move on, you lazy boys," they were told by one of the girls who had been keeping pace with Angela and Melissa.

"Who died and put you in charge?" Perry enquired less than delicately. He folded his arms and came over to speak to Angela's group, Melissa shied away and leant against the stone wall met up with the end of the path. JW was over by the tree stump with Jordan talking about how they had met bigfoot. Just then one of the popular girls shrieked.

"Eww, who stepped in dog shit?" Jenny yelped.

"That's a warning," Perry told her, imitating their teacher.

"Oh, hilarious," she snipped at him in reply.

"How come she didn't say *I have a boyfriend*?" James mocked her hardly trying to hide his comment under his breath. Her blonde eyebrows narrowed but she turned away from the boys.

"Probably because she's a lesbian now," Melissa could hear Jordan hiss to his friends around the stump.

"Dude, harsh as fuck," James laughed. JW smiled but failed to see the humour in the comment from Melissa's point of view. "Although, everyone knows lesbians are hot as hell..." he added and the group of boys all laughed even more.

"I don't get it," Samantha told them, folding her arms over her chest as she stomped away.

"Why doesn't anyone admit that they stepped in poop?" Melissa could hear Jenny ask her equally athletic, tall, blond friend.

"It was probably Melissa," Samantha shrugged nastily.

"Ugh," Melissa grumbled to herself blushing. She checked her shoes discreetly and they were clean.

"Oh bugger it was me," she heard Jenny comment later on as they walked back to the changing rooms about another three laps and forty minutes later.

It was at lunch the next day. Melissa was laid under the oak tree in front of the school with her Book of Shadows lying on her bag nearby while she herself lay down inside her warm winter coat. Louise was walking away to buy chips for lunch and Melissa had not eaten anything yet. She felt a hunger pang at the thought of eating chips, her potato cravings coming on, but her stomach knew by now Melissa never ate lunch usually. As she was lying there pondering her lack of appetite JW zoomed past on his bike. The gust of wind and dust he brought up in his wake disturbed her book. The damp wind was a light breeze until all of a sudden the pages blew in a mad flurry. Before this the wind hadn't been strong enough to pick a leaf up. The pages stopped blowing when they reached- *my True Love spell!* Melissa gasped as she looked up at the sky and muttered, "Mammy?" She hugged the book to her chest. On the front of the book it said: *Melissa C. Galloway*, and where Louise had written *'if you touch this I will kill you. Seriously!'* then also some cartoons, mainly of knifes and blood and words from *'Keep out'* to *'I will kill!'* again, written by Louise. Melissa smiled as she wrote, remembering the time Louise had written those things. They were apparently, book protections, to stop other people from wanting to read it. She thought about her crush again, not even factoring in if Louise might read this book, she had gathered for a while. Her friend had been in her life for so long there was hardly any secrets between them. It was more a matter of making her believe those secrets.

Tuesday ~~21st~~ 26th February

I don't know why I should like him so much maybe I just feel sorry for him or I just like him because I do, but the only question I have is this, dose he like me as much as I like him?. Mum any advice? I imagine saying this to the picture of my mammy placed in the middle of my alter, she had been so unlike my dad, I missed my mum but so far she's just another thing I've lost. -MG

She placed the book inside her bag when she was finished writing and stood up. She went for a walk around the school to stave off hunger. When she was done walking she returned to the spot by the oak tree to rest until the end of lunchtime.

When JW returned from his lunch Melissa quickly hid behind the wall of the school building beside the fire escape for the technical department on the Southeast exit from the school's main building. While JW locked up his bike in the bike cages he chatted casually to his tall red haired friend James.

She watched them silently. Curious about their conversation. She might as well have been invisible to him then. Melissa was aware people were talking about her a lot. There was one thing there she had an advantage over them. She knew the truth and that was important. In a lot of ways over the last year's school she had grown and matured. She had the confidence to speak to JW at times. Other times, it was better she were invisible. Her stomach grumbled then.

"Melissa!" JW shouted there, as if he had the tempus motum ability had appeared in front of her. Like an apparition so she failed to look at him.

"I'm fine," she insisted. Predicting his concern.

"Girl, do you not eat?" James asked her then.

"Louise got me chips again," she lied, so her stomach betrayed her.

"For fuck sake," JW cringed away as Melissa collapsed onto the gravel in front of them.

"Did she faint again?" Melissa heard while she was carried into the school. People whispered as the big strong physical education teacher carried her through the doors.

"Did I have another premonition?" she asked herself, wishing her Dad could explain it to her.

"No, she just hasn't been eating properly," she could hear Louise whispering from a far since her consciousness was fading again.

Richard was worried, immeasurably so, he was worried enough to leave work in the middle of the day during a weekday - almost alien for him. He had been called in to collect Melissa from school. It was stressful and he did not want to do it again after only being there for parents evening a month and a half ago. He had to get the bus there and miss half a day's work because the nurse insisted he take her home. He would be able to work from home though, so it was not a complete loss.

"Fuckin, bugger, fuck," JW sighed as he was forced to wait in reprographics as he let his anger get away with him. This was a similar feeling to the time that he had been called by the wrong name that first time in German class. He knew he had to calm down and stop swearing. However, it felt terrible that people were already accusing him of hitting Melissa and putting her in this sorry state. It had taken all of ten minutes for Samantha to see him come in late to PSE in the huts with Mr Wallace, explain to them why James had ran to get someone to carry Melissa inside and get Louise. She and Jenny just waltz up to him and straight up disdainful accused him of putting Melissa into a coma.

"A coma?!" He had roared, "Are you girls actually that ducking stupid?" He thought he had said but apparently it was much worse. His memory got foggy there. He had anger issues, it was something that most teenagers dealt with. Yet, he seemed to be the only one of the boys in their class constantly throwing tantrums.

"Ugh, I hate this school," he groaned and sat in the small hovel where he was sent to calm down. He was glad to have friends. James always backed him up, Jordan understood him and Perry was a constant ally at times. He was unbelievable thankful for his friends, since being an outcast most of his life because of his family, or nationality, or to put it simply just because he spoke differently.

"Hey, um so I was supposed to be in Art right now, right?" He looked up and saw Melissa stood in the corridor. She was indeed correct, as everyone else was in class, the corridor beside them was completely empty.

"W-what are you doing here? You were taken up to the nurse's office," JW stuttered, trying his best not to hyperventilate. "Hey are you ok?" He asked her with a little more consideration.

"Oh I have my ways," she chuckled and sat beside him on the chairs. "What you doing out here, didn't your Regi class have Mr Wallace now?"

"Got sent out on account of an outburst at Samantha," JW chuckled anxiously.

"Oh, I bet she did something to deserve it."

"She accused me of punching you into a coma, actually," He replied nervously.

"Yikes," she giggled and playfully punched him in the arm.

"Tell me the truth Mel, how come you let people think you're a weirdo and don't care? I mean. It makes me so angry," JW muttered, clenching his fists. She considered it.

"Huh, is that actually what you think?"

"Yeah," he glanced at her and she was blushing. "Do you not realise that people think that of you?"

"I'm only a first year, I'm self-conscious, and I use my shyness to hide my insecurities I guess," Melissa shrugged. "Anyway, for some reason my Dad is here, I better go see what's up," she said and then bolted. JW watched her almost running-jogging away down the red hallway. Her Hooch trousers were still gorgeous on her, even covered in gravel and dewy grass stains.

"I'm insecure too," He sighed. He took a couple of deep breaths and then sauntered back to the huts for his class. He prayed silently nobody said anything about his absence.

Chapter Fifteen

8th August 2001

Melinda was initiated last week. With her Mum leading as the High Priestess. Her hair was tied back in a decorative mass of curls and she had a beautiful robe on- she looked like the Goddess herself.

I gave her a small statuette of the Greek Goddess Venus as a commemorative gift. She appreciated it very well. Then, today, I was alone with her in my car. We drove to the Market in Elgin and had to collect her little sister from there where she had a drama group in the town hall. She sat quietly in the back the whole car ride. Alison Barnes has not a single friend in the world except her sister.

"I don't want to go to the market with him, he *feels weird*," Alison moaned. Stupid empath, and they haven't even noticed it yet.

"But Grandma will be there," Melinda told her brightly. The lovely Naomi Barnes who hated my guts. I didn't want to go to the market either.

"Adrian Turner is bringing her granddaughter, Erin, as well, I heard," I told the two girls in my car. They both smiled at the same time and expressed their jubilation. Adrian Turner was like their third Grandmother. She had been their High Priestess before retiring and their Mum had taken the reigns. Unlike them, I didn't see the excitement.

Adrian is extremely superstitious and has produced pretty dire offspring. Erin is the only Grandchild who inherited her power or interest in the occult. Her daughter, I have been told, had a difficult life. To me it seems she cannot do the simplest spell and cannot keep a man because of it. It doesn't help her case the coven is against all forms of love spells and contraceptive sex spells. Oops? I guess I'm a bad boy?

Melinda cringed at the last part of what she was reading. Having stolen a few pages from Quentin's book of shadows she was reading them in order to remind herself of his version of the events in the last year. It hurt her to know he had done things to her, and drugged her, but the way he wrote he seemed completely unlike the person whom she had grown up with.

"Quinten," she hissed and tucked the torn page under her mattress where she kept it hidden. She moved on to reading the next entry of his diary she had stolen. Thankfully, the dark spells were obvious so any of those she had accidently torn from the book she could discard of immediately. The only reason she kept those was to decipher exactly what drugs he had used on her.

"Big Sis?" she heard her younger sister at the door of the bedroom they shared. Alison was an emotional child and she was also perceptive. Melissa always thought it was something little girls were like, but from the words she was reading perhaps there was more magick to the child's plight.

"I'm just doing my homework, come back later," she lied, trying her best to keep her voice level. It was hard these days. Since she had been diagnosed with depression her family were more aware of her wanting to be left alone at times. Alison would understand when she was a teenager, they all thought.

"Okay," the little girl whimpered through the door. Her older sister listened out with bated breath until she had shuffled away from the closed door. Melinda bit her lip and lay down on her bed. The springs absorbed the tension in her body as she relaxed. The sheets were her best friends- it had been a while since she had thought of her friends from school let alone did homework. The Steiner school were way too understandable and was frustrating because for every day she spent on depression they still charged her parents for her to attend again when she was feeling up to it.

"I'm sorry," Melinda whispered more to herself because she knew her family could not possibly hear her. She knew stealing was wrong but his actions proved his secrecy was horribly in need of retribution. The threefold law would have to requite it eventually, and, after all, the child psychologist from the Rowan centre encouraged her to seek out her own means of recovery. Reading these disgusting book of shadows entries were her methods of coping. Although, this was a twisted form of self-therapy.

30th August 2001

Today I met Erin at a shop in Inverness. We talked for a while in Waterstones. I bought her a book on Glamour's and she took it gratefully, as if it was her life force. She is a book magnet and adores reading. Adrian has a library in their attic, I know from visiting them for the coven meetings at; I offered her a lift home because she lives far out and has no buses directly to her house. She accepted because it was too cold to wait in the bus station, and dangerous, by herself at age thirteen. She walked to my car, where she looked at it with disdain, I don't know why. She complained about the (Scottish) cold weather so I suggested she warmed her hands on the heater.

Erin is a pretty thing. Soft, gentle, pale and skinny, just like her grandmother. She is the daughter of Shona and Byrne, the first grandchild of Adrian Turner, part of a family with deep magickal routes that goes back hundreds of generations. As I drove her home she explained a lot about her upbringing. She inherited a family trait for hoarding knowledge ever since they had to rebuild their house years ago.

A huge fire broke out one Yuletide and it burnt their mansion to the ground. Unfortunately, she lost her father, Byrne, and paternal grandfather in the fire. Only the women and children who survived it. Could have been the arsonist's plan, I speculated. I believed it could have been Shona's jealous ex-husband because since then he apparently went to prison for manslaughter. Erin went to boarding school and her family stayed in sheltered housing in the Highlands until they could go back to their family estate.

In my loosely objective opinion it's Shona's fault. She keeps bringing children and new partners into the mix and it screws up the lives of the pre-existing children and evidently her older relatives. As a result she is also a right superstitious person. Her mother is also extremely superstitious... Erin is the only one of her many siblings who has an inkling of power.

Melinda sighed. She could read into the meaning behind his words. Quentin had his eye on Erin Juligué. She had no idea they had ever spent time alone together, this was concerning. She gasped, swiftly aware of how things had altered since she had read his book of shadows. Sometimes secrets were better left unknown.

"Melinda Naomi Barnes. If you don't answer me I'm coming in," came the voice of her concerned mother through the bedroom door. Melinda panicked and hid the pages under her mattress out of sight quickly. Her heart was beating fast as she sat on the bed just when her mother burst into the room. She made the bed covers flat so her parent could sit beside her, their eyes meeting for the first time all afternoon.

"Hi Mum," she mumbled, knowing she was in for another serious chat about her mental health.

"So, how can you do homework if you haven't been to school? Is this right, my bonny lass?" her mother enquired raising a brown wispy eyebrow at her. "Alison said she sensed you were feeling unsure," Her mother said, with a hesitant tone. She hooked her ankles together as they dangled when she slouched back on the bed to lean against the wall. The cut-out pictures of her daughter and friends from the Steiner school, surrounded by paper hearts, gave her a feeling of nostalgia from her youth. In fact most of the bedroom was much like hers was in university accommodation. There were posters, crafty scrap-bookings, and abstract paintings. The only thing missing was a bunch of Hippie accessories. A lava lamp and rainbow bead curtains would sit nicely. The walls themselves were a deep red with black stripes on the skirting boards. They matching the bedding and the curtains which were a similar pattern yet with darker burgundy. Alison's bed had childish sheets from the Little Mermaid- Ariel was her favourite Disney Princess and she had spent a few years wishing to become either a mermaid or a singer. Melinda's mother sighed, her black clad figure curving into the shape of the bed as she sunk lower until she was lying down with her hips hanging from the bed. She sank onto the floor from this position with a small thump.

"Well Mum, you're not setting a great example," Her teenage daughter said to her, looking down at her from the bed. She tilted her head up to look at her.

"I'm just trying to get comfortable, would you meditate with me for a little while and then we'll talk about how your appointment at the doctor went today."

"Okay, okay, but only to make sure you know I'm trying," Melinda sighed, hunching her shoulders. She scrambled onto the floor and sat cross legged facing her mother. Her Mother, who tried her best to understand depression, but still could not grasp it. Their family shared a lot of things, but darkness in a person's heart like depression was a thing they thought could be dealt with through meditation. As a history of empaths, negative emotions were easily found and snuffed out. Maybe if Quentin is right, Melinda thought, my little sister will help to cure me... she hoped it was possible, but just now the voice in her head was convinced it was impossible.

"Relax your mind, close your eyes and take ten slow deep breaths," her mother began leading them both into the meditation. "Count your breaths. Now you're settled in, turn your attention to your breath. Just place the attention on your breath as it comes in, and follow it through your nose all the way down to your lungs."

Melinda followed the instructions, feeling her mind become blank and less troubled as her consciousness floated away. Adapting to a guided meditation was old hat to her. Attending sabots and countless circle gatherings had made her, and the rest of her family, almost expert at letting go into meditation.

"Breath, let your mind lose track of all your living worries," Her mother said, and it did, it helped. It let her free to wonder how other witches were faring, as if she could astral project into their lives and see how their powers were progressing.

Chapter Sixteen

Melissa knew she was going to be late to school. She woke up after her Dad had left for work- he walked to get the bus early as they didn't have a car- so she got dressed and came downstairs into the kitchen and ate a yogurt with Crunchy Nut cereal at the breakfast table by herself. She realised she would not be capable to walk to school in the time she had left to get there and decided to use her special power. After she had brushed her teeth and laced her shoes on, she used it... erratically pondering on a better name than *Tempus momentum* or *Tempus rerum imperator...* She concentrated on a location near the school would most likely be deserted during the half hour before Registration started.

She appeared in shimmering blue and white crystals, in behind the oldest oak tree in Sanquhar woods. No one could see her when she came out of the woodlands, nor when she ran around the back of the school past the Basketball court and the car park.

As she walked anxiously around the bike cages she was almost run over by JW on his mountain bike. He cursed loudly as he was forced to break hard. When it happened the world went into slow motion and Melissa almost collapsed from shock. She had an epiphany of the bike making impact and imagined how it would have hurt and bruised her. Thankfully it had not been that drastic. He skidded to an abrupt stop, his brakes screeching in complaint, and watched as she fell over. On that day Melissa was wearing blue jeans and a pink top over a grey long sleeved t-shirt. JW was wearing his black hooded jacket and grey jeans with holes in the knees. When Melissa sat up she slowly looked up at him, drinking in his whole outfit. Their eyes met and she could see his confusion then he looked back and she stood up and he push walked with his mountain bike to put his bike away.

For five seconds I held his gaze, for five damned seconds, Melissa thought, pitying herself. She speed walked to her registration class to meet up with Chloe and Alisha by the end of the English corridor.

"Good morning! Well don't you look startled, we thought you were going to be off," Alisha said cheerily.

"Morning... I almost was," Melissa muttered in reply, following the two girls into class where they sat down with Johanna. Both had their brunette hair tied up. Today Melissa found out her registration class teacher would be taking her class for English. Usually they had Mrs Brown up at the end of the English corridor, at the doors leading to the library, but today she had called in sick at 8am. So Melissa was told to come to the same room as registration instead of the normal English classroom. Melissa liked Mrs G. she had a red BMW beetle and like most teachers an obsession with old songs. She always seemed like she enjoyed teaching in comparison to their registration teacher who had a scary aura and an even weirder classroom...

"Right class, I've decided you're going to do a bit of reading ahead of when I take you for your second year," The entire F class groaned as the play in question was handed out to everyone. She did not explain why her walls were covered with black paper and had

182

ignored the stares the pupils gave her as they had filtered into the small class. It was about a third the size of Mrs Brown's room, thus she let them sit anywhere they pleased. It turned out was just what she did with any students- contrary to strict German Language teachers like Miss Duvall who took great care into placing students.

The class had an out of character polite murmur as they accepted the texts in a mannerly fashion. Presumably, they were intimidated by their substitute teacher into being model students.

"Please volunteer to read parts or I will give them at random," She said as the class received their copies of Shakespeare's light hearted love story play, A Midsummer's Night's Dream. "Don't be daunted if you can't understand it, I won't expect you to right now." She went on, "Your first term we will read this play together in full and then you will each write about it."

"What's with the deco?" James asked Jordan in a hushed voice.

"Oh yeah, meet my older brother Matt," he joked.

"What?" gasped Jenny, turning around to look at the plastic figurine hung above their temporary English teacher's desk; it was a shrunken head with a sign underneath it reading "Do your Homework!" in a bold chiller font.

"That's what happens to pupils who don't do their homework," The teacher explained, looking dead serious. The class members who had never met her before gasped. Melissa's friends from Registration rolled their eyes quietly.

"I bet she's a witch like Melissa," Perry hissed to JW, who didn't offer a reply.

"Since nobody volunteered I'll decide, you'll each learn a part and then read it to Mrs Brown in your next class when you get her again. Please don't worry if it doesn't make any sense, in your second year you'll be learning the scripts in a lot more details. I just want to emphasise that," Mrs Harris declared, giving the pale boy a stern look as she spoke before her eyes fell on the table in front of her where the scrawny Atkinson boy was sharing his book with a ginger boy. To her curious surprise he was reading the cast descriptors.

"Oh-oh! Can I please be Puck?" Jordan exclaimed.

"Oh! Me too!" James piped in. They both waved their hands in the air and were hopping about in their seats energetically.

"Fine! So long as you each choose a different part to read," Mrs Harris sighed. She judged James and Jordan were both terrors and longed to just get past this fifty minute period without swearing at them. Craving for a coffee break or something stronger.

"Yay!" the collective voices echoed.

"You can't ALL be Puck!" The teacher sighed with exasperation and defeat. "Just these two idiots," she pointed.

"Oh get in!" Jordan cheered, held up his hand palm open for a high five. James reacted with a heavy and loud slap which could be heard from the corridor.

"Belter!" James said as the glorious smack connected.

"Melissa, your turn to speak," Mrs Brown instructed kindly during the next English class when they were back in their main classroom. The big windows brought a lot of the afternoon light into the room, casting it across her teacher's desk creating a golden glow around her coffee mug. It lit up the children's hair with a red halo-especially on the ones with hair like James.

Melissa spoke softly and quietly when she stood up. Planning to do her best to project her voice, although it came out as a lilting whimper. Subtle hints of an accent to her voice could be noted as she read out loud. Mrs Brown was unsure of just what was happening. She could barely hear the poor girl over the whispers and snickers in the classroom yet she had to resist the urge to clap at how poetic the poor girl was, but instead smiled and gave nods to encourage her, as if it came natural to her to speak with a Shakespearean voice. She spoke an entire page of the soliloquy from A Midsummer's Night's Dream without a single stumble, or stutter, and aside from clearly being aware she was being talked about by her classmates Melissa seemed to find her confidence in the text - as if she had become Hermia completely. It was of no importance to Mrs Brown to know what other things were going on outside class. To her what was important was this soliloquy could be used to give credits for Melissa on her report cards. It would help her to know she had performed with confidence. She felt a swell of pride as she wrote down the grade.

"Now, on the subject of next year you'll be put into English classes which match the grades for this year. For all of you, you'll be pleased to know, isn't so different. Thank you all who performed in the class today from your lesson with Mrs Harris on A Midsummer Night's Dream, by William Shakespeare. Those who did not perform today, I look forward to your class talks on your chosen subject."

The class members who she directed her words to looked away apprehensively and envied those who were excused from class talks.

Mrs Brown stood up, and as she addressed the class had her eyes on the class clock.

"Those who have their talks yet to do I would like to know your chosen subject by the end of class on Friday. As for now feel free to pack away your jotters and pencil cases," Mrs Brown said with a smile, the class joined her as they counted the seconds down to ten twenty-five. The school bell rang signalling the morning break and she dismissed the class. Without another moment's delay Mrs Brown grabbed her cold coffee mug and sprinted to the Teacher's Lounge to brew herself a fresh one.

They had to prepare two minutes on a subject of their choosing. Girls found this easier than most- there was a girl in their class who took archery lessons and Jenny and her friends elected to share the efforts on their individual talks by each showing different aspects of their favourite sports but researching in the library together. James was doing a talk on mountain biking and his friend Scott was doing a talk on Rugby. Expensing of the obvious- Perry talking about Olympic swimming; JW was the only one of the boys who had chosen to do a talk on something vaguely creative. Although, he kept to himself until he had thought of what it was... in the end he chose to explain why he wanted to be a forensic scientist when he grew up.

"One of my inspirations for choosing this career path is Comic book related. The Flash is a forensic scientist," JW explained during his talk the next week. Samantha and a few of his classmates scoffed. Mrs Brown shushed them and encouraged him to carry on.

"I didn't know that about the Flash," she added.

"Yeah, it's not just his super speed but his super intelligence. He is able to use his speed to his advantage solving cases and fighting crime. The Flash, among many crime fighting comic heroes, was my inspiration for wanting to study science. Not many people would know but it needs an in depth knowledge of biology and chemistry to do. Also there are jobs available and areas to study all over the world. Europe, America and all across Asian continents have the best technology for forensic science."

"Wow, you must be passionate about it," the teacher gasped. She listened to his talk with some piqued interest. After the other boys in first year it was a relief to meet one with a mature intelligence. She wondered if there was a reason for JW's advanced intellect for his age, but it didn't matter so long as he had his high grades to pass the year and go on to study Credit level with his classmates. He would fly through school- Mrs Brown smiled. She adored her students and felt highly of them.

"NERD!" Samantha screamed at JW later on as they left their English class after school.

Melissa had déjà vu as she watched the exchange. She flicked her hand and actioned for Samantha to slow down. The Goddess allowed something to happen- Samantha turned around with a confused expression.

"What are you doing here?" she asked Melissa with an accusatory glare. "Huh?"

"Shouldn't you be going home?" Louise's voice declared as she strutted into the group of blondes and stood in front of her best friend, protecting her from the popular girls.

"Let's just go," Jenny begged her friend, also confused about what had happened. To her it looked as if Samantha had stopped moving for a couple of seconds- people were ogling them and sniggering just a bit too much for her liking.

"Ok! Let's leave the weirdos alone," Samantha shrugged off her friend and the popular girls strolled tersely through the library exit. Louise turned around to see Melissa and JW stood side by side. She smiled at them knowingly.

"Time to go home. My cousin David wants to give me a present for my birthday this weekend."

"Okay Louise," Melissa nodded. She turned to say goodbye to JW however he was already gone. Louise frowned and took her hand to guide her through the corridor.

"Hey that was rude!" Louise called after him, he marched through the crowd of students towards the corridor where his locker was to get his things. "You could thank us for helping you!" she demanded of him, knowing full well he could hear her but he was just choosing to ignore her.

"Let it go, Lou, he's not interested," Melissa reasoned, not upset by having her hand yanked she let her friend plot the course.

"I will not *let it go!* We just helped him from a bad situation, if we had not helped he might have thrown a tantrum again or actually hit her. Do you not hear about the thing what happened in Mr Wallace's PSE hut? He's just, ugh, you know?" Louise fumed, as JW made it out of the doors and away from her just in time. She sighed and let go of Melissa's hand so they could walk side by side from the school. It was yet another brisk March day, although the weather was better than it had been- it did rain that afternoon. They had been able to come to school without suffering the inconvenience of carrying heavy winter coats. The air smelled warmly as well, a mix of teenage sweat and other body odours, but mostly of an earthy nature smell of fresh rain. The atmosphere was also quiet- there was a gentle stream in the river Mosset by their side under the murmur of tired Academy age school children. They walked along the dirt footpath on the side of the river. Louise talked mostly about school, leading the conversation, Melissa mumbled a response when it was required of her. Until They both saw the boys wiz past on their mountain bikes.

"What was he?" Louise abruptly gasped, screwing her fists tightly around her school bag straps. "I mean, who does he think he is? He could have at least said goodbye to us! Geez," she clarified, walking faster to get down the road where they would meet up with her younger cousin David. She stomped out her frustration, muttering to Melissa as she went. "Melissa, do you think JW is avoiding me for some reason?" she snapped then, looking Melissa in the eye. They went from the path to the road and had made it past a few houses along the road without having to stop to let a car go past them. Burdshaugh road was not deserted as many students from the academy walked along it to get to their own houses.

Melissa glanced at her feet, "Umm I dunno, I don't see why he would," she tried, her shoes were dirty she noticed. Louise liked to wear white Hogan's were a popular brand in their high school. Everyone who was vaguely popular would wear the same expensive brand of high-top trainers, as well as Helly Hansen jackets and raincoats to school. It was the biggest craze. Louise's trainers were thick with an oversized tongue dwarfed the laces; Melissa thought it looked like it had suffered a severe allergic reaction to peanuts during its manufacture process. Her shoes were typical shop bought shoes from the local Forres shoe store. Although, she did own a pair of brand converses that had seen better days- second hand and from her younger cousins of course (she had tiny feet). Louise poked her in the arm to stir her into sense.

"Like he doesn't say hi to me at all, I don't know what happened or what I did to make him not talk to me," Louise whined. She prodded Melissa to make certain she was tuning in.

"I don't know, I can't say I've noticed," Melissa admitted honestly. She was used to a bitching session from her best friend by now. Louise FM was her favourite show, in fact it was the only show, aside from MFR, and she listened to in reality. She smiled at her own joke inside her head.

"I think in fact he only speaks to me around you or Jordan, *in fact* maybe Jordan is his new master. At least be thankful he still speaks to you," she huffed flicking her hair.

"Um, ok," Melissa shrugged, she met eyes with the small Primary Seven boy as he approached them in his Applegrove Primary school sweater and black polyester trousers. "He's not a dog, you know right," Melissa said just as David had joined up with the two older girls. He smiled at them both and stuck out his tongue.

"Woof, woof!" David yapped, imitating a golden retriever.

"Yes dear, that's nice," His older cousin rolled her eyes at him as she spoke. He gave a small whimper and puppy dog eyes.

"I thought you were funny," Melissa told him, patting him on the head. He yapped with pleasure and she patted him again, then he had to do a few more hops and jumps before the girls got bored of his acting. "Anyway," Melissa said, gesturing to Louise to continue her rant. David faded back into something resembling a human boy, behind them with some of his school friends.

"You know I used to think JW was a smoker because I saw him go up the hill where the smokers hung out, I bet you'll know, if he was, but you know I don't smell it," Louise went on. "You know how much I hate smokers, like you *know*, and I wouldn't want you to have spent the last eh- six months fancying a boy who smokes," Melissa nodded considering what Louise was saying more closely this time, she tapped her hand to her chin. Louise busied herself with her hair as they walked, checking her makeup looked good at the same time using the mirror on her mobile phone. It was built into the back of the case on her Nokia phone.

"I have said before too, but it's apparently not that."

"Please let me know if you ever find out what it is, anyway, David. Did you have my birthday present?" she asked changing the subject as she spun on her Hogan clad heels to face her cousin.

"I'll show you when we get to your place," he told her with a small wink. The group walked home from school and exchanged stories about their days along the way. Once Melissa had seen what her friend's present was she spent the weekend at the Owen's place celebrating her best friend's birthday with a night out with them at a nice restaurant and then a slumber party which followed with just them. It was a small party but still fun. Louise had a few Limousine outings for Birthdays but this year had opted for something a little low key. It had mainly been due to the fact that her brother had been treated to a lot of pre-university shopping trips and as a result her parents had forgotten to book her birthday Limousine ride or even invite her friends. She felt like it was better that she act like an adult-begging for a pair of high heels for her birthday did not help with that. She tried them on when Melissa was over for the first time and showed them off to her younger cousin before he left on Friday after school. The bulk of the Birthday weekend was spent in Louise's bedroom...

As it was the weekend Melissa and Louise were hanging out at Louise's parent's house in Louise's bedroom. After exhausting her extensive collection of romantic comedies, multiplayer computer games, and refusing to approach homework the two girls had decided to read. They were reading a couple of books Louise claimed she had borrowed from her auntie Beatrix.

"Borrowed? These?" Melissa questioned, looking at the black bin bag she had emptied in front of her. Louise kept a bag of Pagan books hidden under her bed and made certain to check the door was closed before she showed them to her best friend. Louise's parents, or her Dad to be more precise, was from a devoted Christian family. This meant she was not supposed to listen to her friend or her auntie. They were decent people but also "crazy" to put it in terms an eleven year old could understand. Melissa recognised Louise often felt patronized by her father and so did not begrudge her desire to be rebellious in this particular way. After all, they were only books to her.

"Yeah, of course," Louise huffed in reply, her hands on her hips as she did a dramatically loud eye roll. Just books, of course.

"Well they're ...um?" Melissa browsed through the titles, biting her lower lip in concern. There was a lot of books. Their titles were somewhat crude compared to the books her Dad and Aunt had given her to study. Graphic gore and nudity danced across their covers. The experience felt similar to watching Adult channels by accident when flipping through Sky for something to watch.

"I'm feeling drawn to these ones the most," Louise murmured, blushing at the covers of the three titles she had picked up and handed them to Melissa who was sat crossed-legged on her bedroom rug.

"I didn't think you believed in Mythical creatures or Beasts from – Native American folklore?"

"It's quite fascinating how the different tribe thingies think," Louise said nonchalantly as she sank into her bean bag chair sat just below her hamster cage. Melissa picked up a book on Algonquian legends called the Book of the Beast's. She flicked through it until she reached a page about the Wendigo psychosis...

"The Wendigo..." she mumbled loud enough for Louise to hear and then fell back onto the rug with a thud. Louise leant forward curiously and sat on top of her friend who was eerily still. She was just about to consider calling her mother through when Melissa sat up with a start and banged her chin on Louise's forehead. Louise briefly reflected she wouldn't have minded performing CPR, mouth-to-mouth, and blushed at the thought. They jumped apart quickly and mumbled embarrassed apologies at each other while Melissa held her chin and Louise held her hand over her own forehead.

"You stopped breathing?" Louise gasped, blinking rapidly with confusion, still cradling her head, still blushing, her bangs poking over the top of her delicate long fingers. As Melissa was about to answer there was a loud eight-bit ringing filling the room. Louise jabbed her free hand into her pocket and brought out her mobile phone. She flipped it open and spoke into the handset.

"Hi Louise!" sang the cheery voice of their childhood friend, Kirsty Ferguson. Melissa seemed to be listening intently, Louise noticed, her head still reeling. It'll probably start swelling soon, she thought, thank god I have a fringe to cover it with.

"Hey Kirsty!" she replied loudly. Melissa smiled silently.

"My mum's just asked me to go to the shops for her so I was thinking you girls will want a break from homework to come give me company? It'll be fun!" her younger friend, who was still in primary seven, asked. Kirsty was too young to have her own mobile so she was calling from her house phone and meant Louise and Melissa could hear the familiar drone of the television from the other end.

"Sure, I guess you'll enjoy being free of Becca's telly time! I'll ask my Mum if is she want's anything and then we'll meet you there," Louise replied, watching Melissa reading the book with her face contorted in pain. After she said goodbye to Kirsty, she hung up, sighed heavily and pocketed her phone. "What was that?" Louise asked, not making eye contact and picking at her nails.

"I'm not completely sure. I saw-," Melissa was pale as a ghost and shivering as she kept her eyes focused on the book. A chill filled the air, Louise knew what was coming and busied herself with going over to feed her hamster. She tried to ignore the chilled feeling seemed to flood the room as Melissa spoke. Her voice wobbled and quivered like fragile glass. .

"I saw, I saw, JW, and that thing- it was horrible..." Melissa cried crawling over to sit in the bean bag chair on her stomach grabbing at the cushions on the floor around her and burying her face in to hide her tears. The hamster made noises as it came up to the bars to look at the two young girls. Melissa was incoherent in her mumbling so Louise slid a finger through the bars to tickle her furry friend encouraging it to eat. The hamster nipped playfully at her knuckle in response.

"That thing?" Louise asked- when her hamster had noticed the food bowl had been refilled- picking up the book from the floor and finding the page immediately.

It talked about how the cannibalistic creature took lives of many people but the picture was a gaunt figure. A mangled cross between human and deer with the ribs jutting out painfully. Thick, ugly, blood dripping from its great, wide, mouth and over its grey, straggly, fur. Antlers rose from its back and upper arms. This was the Wendigo according to how the painting in the book described it. That alone made Louise cringe. Her eyes skimmed over the page.

"Heart of cold?" She read out loud, curiously.

Melissa moved her head as if to nod but her face remained glued into the cushion.

Louise read the pages of the book as she waited for Melissa to finish sobbing...

"Right, I think you need chocolate," Louise declared decisively, her hands on her hips and a smile on her face. Melissa turned around to face her friend and rubbed her eyes.

"Oh yes!" she agreed, smiling brightly through her tear stained face and red swollen eyes.

Louise smiled cautiously as she grabbed her purse.

25th ~~October~~ ~~May~~ March

I was at Louise's house, she had borrowed some books from her auntie who is a witch, some books about mythical creatures. 'Do they exist?' 'How many different kinds are there' and a unique one-of-a-kind, 'Book of the beast's' half of which turns from human and only attack at night, Louise said one was useless, gory front cover though. 'RING' went Louise's mobile, I looked at a page of the 'Book of the Beast's' the first words were

......

'The Wendigo' at the head of the page I read;

'The Wendigo is thought to have been a shunned tribe's person who has begun to eat others of their tribe out of a cultural belief that it will enlighten them with superhuman strength and speed. Their cannibalistic nature changes their genetics, twisting its form, turning them into the horrid creature with a heart of cold and an un-satiable taste for human flesh. This beast though is terrifying, can be killed by fire and only fire, but -'

After that I was pulled away by a premonition which I didn't understand

......

I saw JW. He was running and he looked terrified.

It felt so real, so shocking, so awful!

Then Louise she had been called somewhere. She had to get something from her Mum in the supermarket, and I went with to keep her company, anyway I went home past Jordan's house to get to mine

......

196

I won't tell Louise because I think she thinks this whole Wiccan thing is a joke, just because my dad messed up that spell she did, she should have done it at her house anyway. She also thinks I don't have active powers, just because she has none. -MG

Chapter Seventeen

Forres Academy lunchtime in the afternoon was a dramatic scene. Melissa watched the third years fighting; Perry was getting dragged across the tar of the car park by his hood. Then she saw JW stumbling up the hill into the woods away from their fellow first year classmates. This action decided for her the decision to drop her rucksack under the shade of a tree and follow him. *He goes up here every lunch time*, she thought, *does he go to hang around with the smokers or just to get away from them?* She gasped as she remembered the beast from her vision and realized it was a Wendigo. That might have been overthinking without any proof, but if it was true, was JW... he might know something about it? Or maybe he was secretly feeding it?

That would be creepy; she shivered internally at the thought.

"I've known him for a year and I've only fancied him since Christmas and it's June now any way," she told herself, as she walked stiffly behind him, slowly. Without warning the speaker on her mobile phone started playing. At first, she did not notice, but as it was playing Atomic Kitten: Eternal Flame, she avoided answering- knowing it was Louise. She tried her best to nudge it quiet but instead it got louder so he heard it too then he tripped and tumbled backwards on top of her.

"Younk!" he squeaked when he landed. Thanks to him they had both toppled down the hill, out of surprise, and were both caked in mud. Luckily, the hill hadn't been too steep. Normally, these things never happened, but if anyone saw them like this together (Perry) would come and see the scene and blab about nothing. Melissa laughed out loud despite the fact his weight was crushing her legs.

"I thought it's a good thing we weren't completely covered in mud, actually though just some bark for me, you know? But on the other hand you're completely covered," she glanced at his trousers and then quickly back up. "In mud, I mean," she added with a nervous giggle. JW lay still on top of her as he felt her breasts jiggle with her laughing. He felt blood rush to his face too.

"Hey, Melissa, you, uh, keep popping up around here, don't you?" he remarked, equally as nervous and shy. She thought he was obviously uncomfortable with talking to her, *maybe it was because he hates me* she immediately assumed and frowned.

"I would have forced a fake smile but like I've read somewhere the eyes are the gateway to the soul. In most people I can read them like a book but you must be written it Greek or something, cause I can read a bit in Latin too, it's what I learnt, the schools here don't ever teach Latin," she rambled, wishing he would get off of her.

"Come on, that doesn't even make sense. What do you mean? Are you saying my eyes don't make sense to you?" he asked, carefully extracting himself from his warm cushion. He purposefully had his back to her still as he looked over his dirty clothes. He would have to explain his sorry state to his Mother when he got home. That would be fun, he reckoned, although feeling bitter about it. He liked these jeans and now he'd have to wear something else to school instead.

"Sorry, I just meant, well I don't know what I meant."

"Could you tell me, please, is it a comment about my anger issues? Unless you haven't noticed we have both been getting picked on in the last couple of months? I'm frankly surprised you haven't picked up on it at all," he began ranting sarcastically. "I'm sorry, I see you are struggling too, obviously it's why you're not eating and causing your health issues, but it's fucking dramatic. Everyone saying these things about you, about me, it's insane. As well as anger, I feel other things too, things I don't get. It's like you're, I don't know, immune to all this stuff around you somehow, and I'll tell you it's not only anger that I'm feeling, it's something else."

"Oh," Melissa blushed, she thought about her Wendigo premonition and a tear came to her eye. It was too much to see it all again even without it actually happening.

"Well you-, you know what never mind, you wouldn't care any way." He finished and turned to leave.

While he stomped away she grimaced and whispered more to herself. "Yes I would," and sat on the grassy bank. JW kept on walking.

After school that day on the way home Melissa was waiting beside her best friend for getting something out of Louise's bag to show her half cousin.

"A snow globe? Wicked!" David beamed. He took his birthday present and held it in the light; he admired the glittery sparkles and gave it a good shake. Inside was a silver fairy, sitting delicately with her wings apart and her knees together, ladylike and mysteriously coy at the same time. The outside edges of the stand were also silver with glittery purple gemstones around the base.

"Yeah, Melissa helped me pick it out at the shop in town, she has an eye for pretty things too," the blonde admitted with a wink. The younger boy hugged the girls briefly. "I've got one just like it too, they can be sisters," she added after they had finished hugging.

"Aw thanks for the present you guys, I'd almost thought you'd forgotten my birthday! What with being such cool academy swots, and being all teenagery," He teased them.

"Hey, we're not swots, have a heart," Louise defended touching a hand to her chest. "Well, maybe I am, but Mel certainly isn't," she added touching her best friend on the arm.

"Not everyone is good in school," Melissa shrugged.

"Hey, um well if anything this present shows you still remember the little people at the big school," David replied, as he thanked them again he secreted his present. Louise pinched his arm.

"Not that little, are you? Auntie Bea says you've got yourself a little girlfriend, check you out! Player," she said, and he rolled his eyes. Melissa held in a giggle as she noticed they both tended to roll their eyes the same way. It was the Owens family trait to be fluent in sass. They turned to include her more in the conversation.

"Oh leave it; Mel, tell her. Anyway I'm sure it's not big compared to you two's. Asked out Dutch boy yet?"

"Err..." Melissa knew she was expected to blush, stammer and jump on the defensive. However, thinking about him after lunchtime gave her goose bumps. She felt the colour drain from her face.

"Yikes!" the eleven year old gasped, his lip raised like it was caught by a fish hook. He glanced at his older cousin and then back towards her friend, they shared an awkward silence for the next millennia while Melissa over thought and felt the familiar tickle in the back of her throat. When she felt the clap on her arm she knew she could hold it no more. She closed her eyes and sneezed.

The two girls landed with a thud next to the silver fence that outlined the school carpark. Melissa looked up at Louise- she looked gobsmacked- but there was no time for an utterance of her shock. There was a strange noise from up in the Sanquhar woods. They stood quickly, bolted across the tar, along the grass and jumped the fence, then across the road and up the hill into the woods. It was slightly darker, and because of the dewy muck and moss on the ground harder to keep solid footing off the public footpath. They walked and walked following the thuds and the rustling noises. Eventually they made it to a spot where there was a little opening in the sky. The two were alone. Nothing living was around could be seen, not even a random dog walker or a feather critter out for a stroll. The noises they had heard from the carpark stopped. They circled cautiously with their backs to each other. They circled slowly, dower faces, then Louise spoke breaking the silence; she sighed pensively.

"It's quiet," She whispered loudly, reaching for Melissa's outstretched hand and clutching it firmly.

"Far too quiet..." Melissa finished in a louder whisper than her; she squeezed her friend's hand and guided her back to the footpath. She explained her premonition in every detail. As she did so she thought back to a conversation she had with her father the previous night.

"Hey Dad, what's a wendigo?" She had asked Richard Galloway over dinner when she had returned home from Louise's house. Richard gave her a questioning look as he swallowed a large mouthful of spaghetti carbonara. He took a sip of water.

"Why do you ask?"

"Um, well in one of Jordan's video games... I mean our history teacher mentioned it!" She corrected herself quickly, Richard gave her a stoic look.

"So you're saying Jordan's video games, which I disagree with him playing by the way, came up in your history class?"

She blushed and then admitted the truth of where she had seen the beast mentioned; if she had not given up he would have guessed it eventually, she reasoned. He could be perceptive when he wanted to be.

"I wouldn't trust the sorts of books Beatrix has in her collection, she is not of the right hand path and she considers herself a grey witch," Richard looked outside as if to check if she was there watching them through the kitchen window before he shrugged and resumed his composure. "Anyway, a Wendigo is a mythical beast thought up from North Native American, Algonquian lore. It lead to the coining of the medical term Wendigo psychosis, which is a phobia of desiring to eat humans."

"That's not all though right?" Melissa asked hastily. She put down her cutlery and scrutinized her half eaten plate of food. Her father continued to eat- seeming to ruminate on the topic. "Would they appear in Scotland?"

"No!" Richard gasped, he wiped his chin that had a dribble of pasta sauce and then licked his finger. "Silly, Mel. They would only show up in Canada and the North of America if they were real at all. Even then, if people were being eaten in this country it'd be spotted immediately."

"What about the teenage girls who go missing from places like Elgin and Aberdeen? What about those?" Melissa reasoned.

"Eh-hem, those stories are awful tragedies. Although, usually it turns out to be a family dispute and they are found again, or there's a lead such as the time sixteen year old ran away with her teacher."

"We discuss weird things Dad," Melissa mumbled, realising her Dad might not quite believe her either. She elected to change the subject. "Oh eh, we've got cheesecake, right?"

"We sure as heck do, finish your plate and you can have some!" He urged her, and she tried her best to finish her plate of carbonara. The premonition shoved to the back of her mind.

The water reflected the slowly fading sun as it expectedly did so around this time of the day. Jozef Wouters crouched down sprawled out on the unkempt dry hill gazing out at the rippling dark waters of Sanquhar Loch in Forres. Beside him was the mysterious paw print engraved in the mud, he glanced at it, and felt a knot twisting in the pit of his stomach. He knew he needed a level of logical skill for his hopefully, future career, one day. The print had to be an animal. A beast would be something too fictional a guess, and he was eleven years old; practically a teenager, he thought, much too old to assume it was something like a beast.

He soiled his black trousers and navy hooded jumper, as he sat there pondering, it must have been a large dog. "Yes, yes," He muttered furrowing his tanned brow and allowing his boyish fringe to falter into his grey shining eyes. Then he noticed a smell and strange shouting nearby, and moved his face toward the noise first.

If only he knew then what facing towards the noise would bring...

Melissa Galloway and Louise Owens ambled over the short grass toward the entrance to the woodland. They stashed their school bags in a bed of bluebells at the foot of an oak tree.

"What makes you so sure?" Louise asked her darker haired friend while she kicked a pathway ahead, pinecones and dead leaves scuttled out of her way. "Is it your *Powers*?" She then pondered with a sarcastic edge and flicked her hair out so the sunlight trickles through it to make it look red.

"No. I saw him go up here. Now I can prove it if we had enough time to find his school bag but we don't, so shut-up and listen chic," Melissa responded firmly, huffing her dyed black fringe to one side. Her friend never seemed to understand her lately, always dismissing Joe as a Crush while also ignoring the suspicious vibe she got from Sanquhar woods. Melissa bit her lip; they both squinted as the sun shone into their young brown eyes.

"We shouldn't be here. We should be walking home. I could get into a lot of trouble being here with you after school. You always get me into trouble, Melissa," Louise began walking ahead up the hill into the woods after ensuring her school rucksack would not be too harmed. The trees along with the moss underfoot made the day seem darker. Melissa sighed following after her. Louise would never understand the reality of her religion; Wicca and Paganism had been

206

a great refuge for her after everything had happened after her mother's death. Even better once Melissa's father had given up on her and let her follow her own path. Now Melissa could go with the wind, if she wanted.

Louise also had a teacher in Wicca, her mother's sister – but to Melissa they appeared to be lies; they were more about curses and destruction than knowledge had been passed down for centuries of the old religion. Although all she wanted her oldest friend to be happy for a while.

"What is that?" Melissa asked out loud rapidly breaking her stride and sprinting ahead.

"Wait!" Louise called catching up with her and they both stumbled toward JW.

JW jumped up startled recognising who it was. Melissa Galloway a girl who happened to be in all his classes, and her forgettable friend who he had met when he visited another friend from school during a school holiday. They were the guy's next-door neighbours.

"Hi Melissa," he breathed deeply, with a smile turning to face them. The two girls jumped backwards, his eyes flicked nervously from Louise to Melissa. He panted.

"You're such a slow runner..." Louise trailed casually noticing him standing there; he was pretty good looking, drenched in sweat, much more suitable to her; she concluded.

"JW!" Melissa gasped a break in her usually calm voice, her already shaking hand pointing past him at the now close and revolting smell. Louise gasped also covering her mouth and stepping back. Josef turned sharply, almost slipping down the steep hill, to see the beast that made the smell. His face blanched, white as a ghost.

There it stood, glaring at all three of them, the stench of blood and bones radiating to this distance. Its blood coated, dirty, silver, hairy body, and protruding claws with sheds of human skin, gave the impression it would be hungry.

The beast's breath was revolting and Louise wanted to throw up but she knew that she hasn't eaten for a while, since lunch time so it would be mostly dry retch or bile. She hurriedly regarded JW who was pale, ghost white and frozen in fear. Melissa seemed calm and the only one that they could trust to get them out of the situation. This was a good thing but if she really thought of it then an eleven year old being calm in the face of death was disturbing. But it was a sign that Mel had seen this happen in a premonition already a few times. Louise nodded decisively expecting her best friend to have a plan...

"Run!" Melissa screamed as loud as she could, while turning and tripping over Louise as she promptly followed the instructions. JW met eye-lines with the *thing* before he turned and followed them.

They shouted simultaneously getting away from it once it started chasing. JW eventually tripped turning onto his back to try and get up to no avail. Frozen in fear he rustled on the ground. The girls faced each other but gawking at the beast. Its bloodthirsty cold yellow eyes, and its teeth as it opened its mouth slightly to growl and amplify the terror. Melissa looked more at it waiting for something to click in her memory.

Josef scrambled away as it slashed out, he bumped into a large tree to lift onto his feet to avoid its low scratching. Luckily he was young skinny and agile enough to avoid it's attacks. Its claws scooped out mud and then lashed at his face in fury; he got to the ground in time to avoid the attack. It simply scraped a multiple of layers of bark. He clambered around the tree quickly realising it only wanted him right now, probably since he was least vulnerable and made him more venerable, he didn't dare try to understand the intricacy of the beasts mind.

Melissa gasped seeing JW give way and slump onto his back.

"What is that thing?" Louise asked Melissa in a low fearful whisper as she faced her friend. The Beast leapt onto the tree crushing its weaker branches to get to him on the ground. Blood and spit flew from its open maw. It crunched the ground where JW had been. The death ending bite that was narrowly avoided. The forest radiated with heat, quivering and shaking around the being that should not have existed. JW cried with fear. His eyes' growing dark as his fate was sealed. The two girls watching in horror, as they knew that once the beast had fed on the boy they were next. Yet, Melissa was calm.

"Fire! It's afraid of fire!" she shouted with all the certainty she could. "The Wendigo, demon has a heart of cold, eating the hearts of lovers; it can only be killed by flame. Anyone who it scratches will become one if they are no interest to it," Melissa recited from memory her face blank for a moment. "It fears fire we need to find something to scare it with!" she called looking around, Louise gasped as she saw a red lighter under her foot she kicked it over to him.

The Wendigo growled as it hovered over Josef, its putrid breath making him feel faint. It brought one arm out and clawed through both his jumper and his white school shirt underneath. He stretched slightly to grab the lighter, after years of helping his mother with her cigarettes he managed to get it to light, breaking the darkness and baffling the beast. The Wendigo turned to run away, and with its size, toppled down the hill.

"Well, that was strange?" JW gasped as they helped him up. Flakes of dried blood were stuck to his clothes they were thankfully it was not his. He stood up halfway before he was taken by the sudden desire to retch. The girls watched, unable to think of what to do or say, as he vomited down the embankment, hunched over and shaking. He glanced at them when he was finished, his eyes dark and face sallow as he wiped his mouth.

"Where's your school bag?" Louise asked after a minute and a shawl of calm draped over them; as if by her summoning request, his shoulder strapped school bag floated slowly up the hill towards her from further down the embankment. "That totally did not just happen," She squealed in astonishment taking it and passing it to him.

"Some things are just hard to explain," Melissa suggested with a smirk looking JW in the eye. He took his bag confused and amazed by the whole evening. He looked away.

"Ugh, thanks," He grunted holding his nose, he nearly retched again right there realising how close he had come to being gobbled whole. Together they all started walking down to where the girls had left their own school bags at the foot of the hill.

"So, do either of you two know what time it is?" Louise asked Melissa ignoring him as he stared at her, taking her bag up before Melissa could get to hers. *How can you girls be so calm?* He thought.

"I don't have a watch; don't you know what time it is?"

"Don't know, you know I think this is a sign we should have taken getting into Wicca more seriously," She smiled up at him as he glared suspiciously; Melissa shook her head and prodded her in the back annoyed, probably jealous, he was staring at Louise.

"Suppose you could just not mention stuff like this to the others?"

He smiled back and nodded. He didn't mind keeping something as traumatic as that under hat. He just wanted to forget the whole thing and shove it to the back of his head. *What an adventure*, he thought.

"Sure..." he told her smiling and nodding again. Just as long as he guessed the Wendigo was gone. "So what time *is it* then girls?"

"Seriously, you see us do all this and that's your first question?" Louise started laughing at him for no reason at all, other than she was so relieved the whole ordeal was over with. "Do you not have other questions? Like... how did we know you were in trouble?"

"Yeah! Loads of questions, but not starting with that. More like, did you just are you using telekinesis or something?" he laughed, JW ignored the better question and pointed at Louise's school bag.

"What the goddamn hell?" she squealed seeing her snow globe floating out of her school bag and hovering towards her ear just above her shoulder.

"That's twice, you're not imagining it," Melissa whispered to her best friend. She shook the snow globe and handed it back to Louise who watched the glitter inside it fall before she spoke again.

"Okay, so whatever this is you need to teach me how to do it. Like later on, cos right now I feel icky," Louise mumbled, she looked at the snow globe, the silver fairy inside of it appeared to be smiling at her.

"Don't we all?" JW remarked, opening the hole in his clothes revealing his chest. Melissa blushed upon seeing his smooth tanned skin; Louise tilted her head with a satisfied grin. Although, JW was more upset about how to explain this to his mother as they ambled down the hill.

"I could sew it for you," Melissa volunteered once she had regained command of her vocal chords and untied the knot in her tongue. Louise gasped with surprise, walking ahead of them across the road. JW and Melissa darted after her, quickly, to avoid an oncoming car. The blonde giggled quietly to herself, amused.

"Ah! Thanks," JW gawped, finally putting away his bare chest. He looked at his trousers that were covered in mud and his shirt that can hardly be explained away easily for the blood.

"After this we are hopefully friends with him?" Melissa whispered indicating the boy as she jogged down the hill into the school car park after Louise. She gripped her friend's hand in a tight squeeze.

"No, he is still friends with Jordan, and Perry," Louise replied, giving her a squeeze in return before letting go of her hand.

"Jordan's not that bad but, Perry ugh, maybe I should start a list."

"Me too, let's call it the list of people who we would want gone," Louise indicated as they stopped on the other side of the road. Melissa took her book of shadows out of her school bag, turned it to the last page and handed it to Louise.

"Why did the Wendigo attack me?" He asked, his eyes fixed on the girls as they fussed over the book nearby.

"You have anger issues so maybe-" Melissa began to say but Louise nudged her sharply in the ribs.

"I daren't dare try to understand the intricacy of the beasts mind. It was probably just hungry, it's like a cannibal after all," Louise interjected. She held a pen with the book open so that only they could see it, when JW tried to glance they stepped away.

"Why else than that?" Melissa asked him, trying her best to put on a reassuring tone. JW frowned, holding the broken fabric of his shirt closed with one hand as they continued to walk through the school grounds.

"I've hurt many people I care deeply about through my anger issues. Just because you care about someone or have good intentions does not guarantee you're doing the best thing for them."

The girls looked at him with worried expressions then and put away the list they had been working on. As the zip was being pulled closed on Melissa's bag JW removed his shirt. Trying not to blush she took it and watched him as he pulled on his PE t-shirt from inside his school bag.

"Bin it. Sew it. Whatever you want to do," He ordered her, his tone flat. She tilted her head, biting her lip and sighing.

"JW, I'm sorry, I understand that was a..." she trailed off, unsure of how to explain things. *Why am I apologizing? It's not like I'm in control of a freaking wendigo attacking him!*

"I'm out!" he grumbled, marching away, leaving the two girls alone stood outside the PSE huts. The skies above broke out into a grey drizzle.

Chapter Eighteen

23rd September 2001 Mabon

Today I was talking to Melinda in the little B&B in Alves I've been staying at as of late. I think she might be really falling for me- maybe so much that I can take away the two poppets. She mentioned a girl whom attended Forres Academy. "Yes, Melissa Galloway..." it was a passive remark on something Dean Simmons (the little fuckface) had told her, yet it made me snap to attention immediately.

"WHO?!" I gasped, unable to contain myself.

"Do you remember Mr Richard?" She enquired, laughing at my intrigue. I admitted I had and she told me the background. He had a girl with a woman who had so much hidden power and potential yet had the unfortunate upbringing of Catholicism. Without much discussion Melissa had been raised Catholic.. (Christened in a Catholic church instead of a Wiccaning like other little girls in Richard's coven). Until Mrs Galloway died when Melissa was only six, Melinda says, they had no idea Melissa did not know about the coven.

Mr Richard wants to reach out to them again because Melissa is starting to show interest in Wicca. Melinda seems to think he needs his coven now...

Melissa could have extraordinary powers with my guidance...

The pages shook in her hands. Melinda took a moment to realise that she was instead the one shaking. Recognising that this could go on no longer she found a match and burned what she had left hidden under her mattress. She was careful not to wake her family as she carried the objects under her night dress into their little back garden. Once the embers of her tiny fire had died down she buried the evidence.

Smelling her smoke imbued apparition afterwards she scurried back into the house - with all the quiet in her steps that did not reflect the noise in her burning mind and pounding heart. Lilting on the landing outside the family bathroom, she stuffed her night clothes in the very bottom of the washing hamper and floated into the shower- either unaware or uncaring of the ungodly hour.

The water cascaded down her smooth milky cafe-lait skin and mahogany brown ringlets. Melinda sighed and held the razor blade in her hand. Her medication had left her feeling numb and catatonic, to the point that Alison, her own baby sister, avoided her. Alison had even asked to have her own room. That was how awful it all was. She felt the familiar ache in her gut as she thought about that. The twinge in her heart. Sister, own flesh and blood, found her depression was too much to handle. Melinda felt the water trickling down between her cleavage and pouted. Her navel had been touched by that jerk. Her beautiful teenage body was damaged and broken beyond repair. She wept.

"What is your plan, oh Goddess? To hurt me?" She whispered, they would be loud guttural sobs if not for the effects of her anti-depressants. Instead she merely sat under the water and letter her tired tears flow. She looked at her arm, fingering the razor again, digging the sharpest area of the blade in until she could feel the fresh sharp sting. Her blood dribbled in a gorgeous deep red inky colour and consistency. Despite all of her horrible thoughts, and what she had read, she felt free. She smiled with contentment.

Turn over for

a Preview of

PART TWO

Second year...

Religious Education

A humid rain pattered against the windows of Mr Nellany's classroom as he read out the names on his register after lunch. The group of secondary school students were celebrating the fact that they were now experiencing second year after all the pampering of first year by experimenting with crafts. He was tall and thin teacher with broad shoulders fit for playing rugby and a face to match. Chiselled jawline and a crooked nose under a pair of brown-gold eyes. He knew for a fact that he was seen as a "cool teacher" because students looked up to him and listened to him. Unlike most Religious Education teachers, who took a solemn Christian view of decorating their classroom, he was over the top with Buddhist decorations due to the fact that he had grown up in Findhorn under holistic new-age views. The lower shelves were lined with hundreds of text books and bibles but the higher up shelves were devoted to little statues and from the rafters were hung colourful flags and motivational quotes. He enjoyed this class from last year despite the fact that bullying was rife among the children. He always kept a close eye on one student in particular. She had a bright young mind and he knew there was something spiritual about her. Melissa enjoyed Mr Nellany's teaching just the same because it was a relaxed style and that made the information sink in and stick. He was one of the few who taught with the students and pupils in mind rather than what the school deemed correct- structured, with robotic answers and all for the sake of results.

"Melissa?" He read out loud then, reading her full name on the roster as *Melissa C. Galloway.* Quietly she called out her presence. He looked up at her again to see the boys picking on her. Again. He would give them a stern talking to as soon as the register was done, they could hold on till that.

He read through the list of names getting to the boy called "JW" although it was written as *Josef A. Wouters* in the register. He smiled knowingly; as they were a second year pupil he knew the whispers and rumours and from looking at how the two children interacted the chemistry was obvious.

"Here!" The young Dutch boy called out as Mr Nellany clicked his pen and marked the roster as complete.

"Just in time, we've marked, everyone is here, one-hundred-percent attendance," He declared standing up to answer the knock on his door. Proudly handing the role sheet from his clipboard off to the janitor who would take the list of students away to the reception office where it would be used in the event of a fire drill or to monitor truancy on file.

"Thanks!" The janitor mumbled swiftly darting away once more. As Mr Nellany twisted left from the closed door he was sure he saw a pair of scissors get launched towards Melissa's face out of the corner of his eye. He spun. Time seemed to slow down around her as she caught the metal implement in mid-air with lightning quick reflexes.

"Jordan?" she squeaked, laughing quietly. Perry sat with his mouth agape. Other students continued with their business undisturbed. He listened to their conversation before he marched back to his desk; it seemed they were just arguing about who was borrowing stationary and not returning it. Nothing out of the ordinary there; they were sharing, lending, and learning all the important stuff about possessions. He would teach them about how that related to Buddhist principles in time.

"Love is not about possession. Love is about appreciation. – Osho said that," Mr Nellany recited to the class from memory, getting a few interested glances in return. He briefly wondered what had happened at the table to initiate the argument, considering they sat at the back left hand corner of the room so he could scarcely hear them. He questioned what he had seen and considered for a moment that it was his coffee consumption.

A moment later JW threw Melissa's purple pencil case across the room, where, as if by magic, it bounced off the wall above the blackboard, back towards her. In slow motion, without anyone turning their heads in shock, the pencil case landed back in her open hands. The teacher dropped into his swivel chair and blinked several times to steady himself before he began the class properly.

"Definitely the coffee," he reasoned, shaking his head.

About the Author

Angelica Murphy-Parker grew up in a small town, in fact the same town in her Tempest series, and it was there she left to pursue other endeavours. She attended college in Aberdeen, moved to study more advanced courses in Ayrshire, close to Glasgow, and travelled haphazardly -to such places as Germany and France- before settling into yet another smaller town to return to her writing passions. Currently she lives in a village called West Kilbride where she enjoys brief sporadic encounters with humanity while also working hard and writing daily.

A wee bit of Geography

Forres lies within the Moray Council area, which stretches from Tomintoul in the south to the shores of the Moray Firth, and then from Keith in the east to Forres in the west. Famous for its colony of dolphins, fabulous beaches, such as Findhorn Bay, and more malt whisky distilleries than anywhere else in Scotland. With the enriching and award winning Benromach distillery situated in Forres itself. Thanks to all of these tourist attractions, Moray is place that thrives with activity all year round.

The council is headquartered in Elgin, the administrative capital of Moray, has to date forty-five hundred grumbling employees who aim to respond to the needs of over ninety-five thousand residents in this beautiful part of Scotland, which nestles between Aberdeenshire and the Highlands.

Scotland is a fantastic country, with vast unexplored locations and an interesting yet colourful history, this makes it an excellent tourist location and setting for any story...